SPECIAL FORCES CADETS

Siege

Look out for
Missing
Justice
Ruthless
Hijack
Assassin

CHRIS RYAN

SPECIAL FORCES CADETS

SIEGE

HOT
KEY
BOOKS

First published as an ebook in 2018
First published in paperback in Great Britain in 2019 by

HOT KEY BOOKS
80–81 Wimpole St, London W1G 9RE
www.hotkeybooks.com

A CIP catalogue record for this book is available from the British Library.

ISBN: 978-1-4714-0725-3
also available as an ebook

1

This book is typeset using Atomik ePublisher
Printed and bound in Great Britain by Clays Ltd, Elcograf S.p.A.

Hot Key Books is an imprint of Bonnier Zaffre Ltd,
part of Bonnier Books UK
www.bonnierbooks.co.uk

1

Striding Edge

It was the weather that changed Max Johnson's life.

Max knew it would be bad, because he knew about clouds. He spent hours staring at them. He knew their names. Cirrus. Altocumulus. Cumulonimbus. And he knew what they predicted. That cold January morning he had seen the high-stacked layers of nimbostratus moving in from the west. 'We shouldn't climb today,' he said to Cory, their team leader. 'A storm's coming.'

But Cory – a hard-bitten climber with a leathery, lined face and a steely grey beard so bushy that you couldn't see his lips – had other things on his mind. He had come down with food poisoning the previous night and was in no state to lead them up the mountain. A gap-year student called Mickey was to take his place. 'Mickey knows what he's doing, lad. He says it's fine.' And Cory quickly took himself back to his sick bed.

Max didn't agree. All his life he had studied his surroundings: the moss on one side of a tree trunk that indicated which direction was north and which was south.

The faint track on a wet path that told him what type of animal had recently passed. The distinctive pattern in the stars of Ursa Major that taught him how to navigate at night. It was hardwired in him to observe. It was part of his DNA.

And his DNA told him that nimbostratus meant a storm was brewing. He voiced his concerns to Mickey, a lanky young man with scruffy hair and a slightly dopey demeanour.

'Nah, I've checked my app,' Mickey reassured him, holding up his phone. 'We'll be up and down in no time. Come on – you don't get a chance like this every day.'

That was true. The cost of this trip to the Lake District was £500. Max was an orphan, and lived in a residential care home in Newcastle. His parents had died when he was a baby. He couldn't even remember them. A social worker had once told him that their house had gone up in flames and the firefighters had to make a choice: Max or his parents. That was all he knew. While the staff in the care home did their best for him, they could never be the family he craved. And there was nobody else. No grandparents, uncles, aunts or cousins to fill in the story of his life or send him presents for Christmas, like the lonely one that had just passed. No family friends to tell him what his mum and dad had looked like, or what sort of people they were. Not even any belongings or photographs. They'd all been destroyed in the fire.

And he had no money, of course. He could never have afforded a trip like this. When Mrs Barclay, the Combined Cadet Force teacher, had told him that his school would pay, Max had gratefully accepted. In fact, he was the most able CCF student at St Andrew's School. He relished what the other kids moaned about – the fitness sessions, the drills, the field trip that had taken them climbing in the Peak District. The tougher the CCF teachers made things, the more Max enjoyed it. That, and living in a care home, made him a bit of a freak at school. Most people went out of their way to avoid him. He spent break times alone and he was never invited to parties. But it didn't bother Max. He was fit, strong and agile and he had a plan: to join the army. It was all he had ever wanted to do. In his dreams, the army would be the family and friends he'd never known. And while a week's climbing in the Lake District was not exactly the German Alpine Guides course that Max knew members of the SAS were sent on, it was still his idea of heaven.

If only he didn't have to put up with the others on the trip – four boys, three girls – who insisted on calling him 'orphan boy' after he'd let slip his circumstances early on the first day. The nasty comments had started immediately. But Max was used to it, and well practised at ignoring insults.

'Hey, orphan boy, nobody wants to sleep next to you in the dorm,' Angus McKay had said that night.

'Hey, orphan boy,' Suze Roberts had smirked as they sat down to dinner, 'bet this is the most food you've seen in a month.'

'Hey, orphan boy, too scared to climb the mountain? It's just a few clouds.' That was Jordan Smith, a lanky kid with a shaved head who seemed to have woken up that morning determined to wind Max up. Jordan was the ringleader. The others all looked up to him.

'Hey, Jordan,' Mickey had said nervously, 'that's not cool.'

Jordan and the others sensed blood. Mickey wasn't much older than the kids he was looking after. Max sighed. He had seen it happen at school whenever a supply teacher took over a class. Inexperienced and desperate to be friendly with the kids, they never stood a chance.

Jordan rolled his eyes.

'Like you'd know what was cool, Mickey Mouse,' Suze said under her breath. The others sniggered. Mickey pretended to laugh along with the joke but couldn't hide his embarrassment. He reminded Max of some of the adults he'd known in the care home. Whenever one of the kids stood up to them, they retreated, snail-like, into their shell.

Now Mickey was pretending not to notice the attitude of Jordan and the others. It made Max more apprehensive about the day. On an expedition, you needed a leader – and Mickey clearly didn't have the respect of the group. He ushered them into the minibus that would take them from the outdoor pursuits centre to the base of Helvellyn. It was the third highest peak in England, and famous for its difficulty.

'Guys, we'll be ascending via Striding Edge,' Mickey announced. 'It's a sharp ridge line that leads directly to the summit. It has a reputation for being dangerous, but as long as you stick with me, you'll be fine.'

'Didn't a couple of climbers die on Striding Edge last week?' Jordan asked. He made spooky ghost noises, then looked around with a grin. Jordan was the kind of kid who liked to scare others.

'There have been accidents,' Mickey said. 'But we'll be all right as long as we're careful and you do what I say at all times.' He caught Max's eye. Max looked away and stared through the minibus window at the darkening clouds up above. 'I've climbed the ridge loads of times,' he heard Mickey say. 'We'll be absolutely fine.'

It was a cold morning. Their minibus was the only one in the car park. The others complained when Mickey insisted they wear waist harnesses and carry heavy loops of climbing rope. They rolled their eyes when he made them share out their supplies and other equipment. It was Max and Suze's turn to carry the foil ration packs that would be their lunch. Angus was given the first aid kit. The satellite phone, for emergency use only, was given to Jordan. 'Doesn't even do Snapchat,' Jordan said, shoving it into his rucksack. Some of the others laughed.

The rain – freezing and relentless – started a few minutes after they set out. It took two hours for them to hike and scramble up the foothills of the mountain. By the time they were approaching Striding Edge, the rain was almost horizontal and Max's hands and feet were numb. Even Jordan was silent as they stopped for a moment and looked at the imposing ridge leading to the summit. It was only a few metres wide. On either side was a steep, scree-covered slope with a drop of at least fifty metres.

'Single file!' Mickey shouted over the noise of the rain. 'I'll lead. Max, you take the rear. Don't let anybody fall behind.'

Jordan brushed past Max. 'Out of my way, orphan boy,' he muttered.

Max ignored him.

The going was slow. The rain was blinding, and the rock was slippery underfoot. Max trod carefully, feeling for loose ground with his walking boots. He tried to avoid looking to either side, but he could still see that the bottom of the slope was invisible, covered in mist and rain haze. Below and to their right there was a mountain tarn, but it was only occasionally visible. Looking down made Max shudder. Instead, he concentrated on the rest of the team snaking out ahead of him. They were the only people on Striding Edge today – with good reason. As far as Max was concerned, the sooner they were back down in the foothills, the better.

It took another ninety slow minutes to reach the summit. It was a bleak, lonely, weather-ravaged place. Max felt none of the satisfaction that he remembered from his previous CCF climbing trip to the Peak District. As the team congregated by a small cairn that marked the summit, he looked back the way they had come. He could see no more than five metres. Striding Edge was lost in cloud.

Normally they would rest for a while and eat something from their ration packs. Today, nobody wanted to do that. Mickey looked anxious. Standing by the cairn, he turned a full circle, as if looking for another descent. The wind howled. It was deafening and very strong, and almost caused Max to lose his footing. He approached Mickey. 'We need to get back down,' he said tersely.

'There are other descents,' Mickey agreed. 'Safer, maybe. But in these clouds . . .'

'We'll get lost?' Max said.

Mickey nodded. 'Maybe you were right,' he said, quietly so the others couldn't hear. 'We shouldn't have come.' He sounded panicky, like he was turning to Max for advice. That was not what Max wanted to hear.

'It doesn't matter now,' Max said. 'We just need to get down.'

Mickey nodded, then turned to the others. 'Guys!' he shouted above the wind. 'The weather's worse than I expected. We're going to make our descent quickly. We'll go back down the same way we came, but this time we'll rope up. The visibility's poor, and this will keep us together as a group. You all have a carabiner on your harness. We'll have five metres of rope between us. I'll lead, Max will take the rear. Does everyone understand?'

Seven bedraggled heads nodded. Only one shook his head. Jordan. 'I'm not roping up,' he said.

'Jordan, you have to,' Mickey said.

'You can't make me,' Jordan retorted. 'You losers rope up if you want. I can get down by myself.' He turned his back on them like a spoiled child.

'Jordan, please . . . It's for your own safety.'

'Shut it.'

'Mate . . .' Mickey started to say, but Jordan stormed off and there was no time to argue with him. The weather was getting worse. Max was shivering. He wished Cory was here. The old climber exuded confidence and capability. Mickey? Not so much. Max noticed that Mickey's hands were slow and awkward as he threaded a length of sturdy blue rope through their harnesses. It took five minutes. During this time, the temperature dropped noticeably. There was a sudden clap of thunder, very close. Mickey looked round again, rain dripping from his face. 'Please tread carefully, everybody.' He sounded exhausted.

Jordan went ahead, not roped up. He clearly had no desire to wait for the others. Mickey looked like he was going to have another go at persuading him, but lost his nerve at the last moment. He followed, and the line of roped-up teenagers snaked behind him. Max watched them disappear into the mist. He could only see one person ahead: Angus. The rope in front of him grew taut and he started his descent.

It was difficult to stay upright. The swirling wind lashed his body from all sides. It was almost like being punched. If Max hadn't known he was on a ridge, he wouldn't have been able to tell. Clouds obscured the sheer drop on either side. He had just started to walk along the ridge when there was another thunderclap. He felt it as much as heard it. The vibrations went straight through him and almost made him lose his footing. Seconds later, a fork of lightning hit the ridge, maybe fifty metres ahead. Momentarily he could see the others, silhouettes in the mist. They disappeared after a fraction of a second. Then all he could see was the mist again, and Angus treading gingerly ahead of him. Angus looked over his shoulder. It was hard to tell because of the rain, but Max thought he might be crying. He didn't blame him. That lightning strike had been too close for comfort. 'It's okay!' Max shouted. 'We'll be down before –'

He didn't get to finish his sentence.

The second lightning strike was much closer. Twenty metres away, if that. He saw the lightning fork strike a boulder halfway along the line of climbers. As it hit, he felt an electric surge run up one leg and down the other.

He called out in surprise and pain, and almost lost his footing again.

Then, above the howling of the wind and the driving rain, he heard a scream. And a fraction of a second later, as a third lightning strike hit, he saw why.

Mickey had fallen. The flash of lightning was just enough for Max to see him tumble to the left, down the side of the ridge. Suze, immediately behind him, was being dragged down. In an instant, Max knew that if he didn't do something, they would all plummet down the rocky slope.

'*JUMP!*' he bellowed at Angus. '*JUMP TO THE RIGHT!*'

It was instinctive. If the others were tumbling to the left, Max knew that his only hope of saving them was to make use of the opposite slope. Grabbing the rope in two hands, he strode to the edge.

There was no time to think. Thinking would just lead to fear. Max threw himself from the ridge, pulling Angus with him.

As Max plummeted though the air into nothingness his stomach lurched, as if he was on a rollercoaster. Then his fall was halted with a horrible jerk as the slack rope tightened. He slammed hard against the wet rock ten metres below the apex of the ridge line. The rope strained. Above him, Angus was shouting in pain and clutching one arm.

Max was battered too. His right side was sore where he had crashed into the rock. But he didn't think he'd broken anything. He could hear panicked shouting, but indistinct above the noise of the storm. He made the mistake of looking down. His legs felt weak as he saw the slope disappearing into the mist and rain.

He tugged on the rope. It was taut but there was no drag. That was good. It meant Mickey, at the other end, was not slipping down the opposite slope. But what should he do? Should he try to scramble up? Or would that mean his weight was not acting as a counterbalance? He hung there, gasping. As the wind and rain battered him, he tried to work out his next move.

Seconds later, his decision was made for him. He slipped a little way down the slope, bumping painfully against the rock. The same happened to Angus, who whimpered in fear.

Max knew what must be happening. Mickey, and whoever else was at the end of the rope, was climbing to the top of the ridge. Max and Angus had to climb too, otherwise they would all slip down this side.

Max grabbed hold of the rope. It was wet and hurt his frozen hands, but he gripped it firmly. Slowly, his muscles burning, he pulled himself up the slope towards Angus: five slow, difficult metres. Angus was still cradling his left arm. He was pale and shivering.

'It's broken,' he whispered as Max drew up alongside him. There was no 'orphan boy' this time.

11

Max looked up. Five metres of rope connected him and Angus. It would be enough for him to use to get up to the ridge. But there wasn't much time. If the others were pulling themselves up, he and Angus would soon slip again.

'It's going to be okay,' Max said. 'But we have to move fast.' He grabbed the rope connecting Angus to the next person along and powered past his companion. There was no time to explain what he was doing. Twenty seconds later, he was on the ridge. He could hear muffled shouts, but there was no sign of the others.

He seized the section of rope leading down to Angus and hauled as hard as he could. He couldn't shift his companion. 'Use your legs!' he shouted. Angus looked up, frightened. '*Your legs!*' Max repeated. Angus nodded. He inched up the slope while Max pulled as hard as he could. It took ten seconds to haul Angus up on to the ridge. Both boys collapsed, breathing heavily.

A crack of thunder. Another hit of lightning. The muffled shouts became more distinct. 'Jordan! *Jordan!*'

Max pushed himself to his feet and helped Angus up. They scrambled towards the top of the ridge. The others came into sight. They were still roped up, but huddled close together. It immediately became clear to Max that Angus wasn't the only casualty. Mickey lay on his back, pale and shivering. His leg was obviously broken – it went off at a strange angle at the knee.

The others looked terrified. A couple were holding their mobile phones, but there was no service. 'Where's Jordan?' Max demanded.

Their body language told him everything. They looked over the edge into the gaping, cloud-filled emptiness beyond.

'He fell,' Suze whispered. 'He lost his balance and he wasn't roped up. There was nothing we could do.'

2

Dülfersitz

'Mountain rescue . . .' Mickey whispered. 'We need mountain rescue.'

Max stared at him. The only way they could make contact with the outside world was by using the satellite phone.

And the sat phone was in Jordan's rucksack.

Max stood up and looked at the slope. The rain was still lashing, and visibility was getting worse.

He put his hands to his mouth. 'Jordan! Can you hear me?'

The others started shouting Jordan's name again, but there was no reply, just the relentless blast of the wind and the rain. They fell silent and peered into the mist. There was no way of knowing how far Jordan had fallen. Fifty metres? A hundred? Was he alive?

There was only one way to find out.

Max realised the others were all looking at him. 'Where did he fall?'

Suze pointed. Max nodded. 'I need the rope,' he said. 'All of it.'

'Max,' Mickey called weakly, 'don't go over the edge. Get to the bottom of the mountain. Call for help then.'

But Max shook his head. 'That could take hours. If Jordan is still alive, he needs help now.'

'What do you care?' Suze asked. 'He was so mean to you.'

'I'm not saying we're going to be best friends,' Max replied. 'Where's that rope?'

They had five loops. Max gathered them up and tied them end to end using secure reef knots. He found a protruding rock near where Jordan had fallen and looped the midpoint of his rope around it. He shouted Jordan's name again. There was no response. With his back to the slope and clutching the double length of rope, he passed it between his legs and round one hip. He then passed it up across his front and over his left shoulder, then round his neck and along his right arm. This was the Dülfersitz abseil position. He'd read about it in books and online. There was just one problem: he'd never done it before.

'First time for everything,' he said under his breath.

'What?' Suze shouted at him.

'Nothing.' He threw the leading end of the rope down the slope with his right hand, and held the anchored end with his left. He let the rope take the weight of his body, then carefully stepped backwards down the slope.

It was steeper than the opposite side. Or maybe it just

seemed that way. Max felt as if he'd left his stomach on the top of the ridge. He gradually let out a little of the rope in his right hand and descended a couple of metres. The rain beat hard against his face and the rope dug painfully into his body. Already the top of the ridge was obscured by mist. And there was no way back up. The only way now was down.

Max tried to shut out the fear, and continued his descent.

A minute passed. There was another crack of thunder. A flash of lightning, uncomfortably close. He called for Jordan. Nothing.

Two minutes.

Three.

He had no way of judging how far he'd descended because he couldn't see more than a few metres in any direction. All he could do was focus on his rhythm: small steps backwards, gently easing out the rope that burned through his wet hands.

At some point he would run out of rope. What then? He had been abseiling for five minutes when his right heel hit a small rocky outcrop. He looked over his shoulder. It was about a metre wide and bulged a little way out from the slope. Max stopped for a moment. This was a precarious spot, especially in this wind. Should he continue descending? Or should he stop here and reset his ropes?

He made the decision to stop. Breathlessly, he unwound the rope from his body. When it was loose, he tugged the right-hand strand. The left strand slid upward. Max kept pulling until finally the entire rope slithered down the mountainside into a heap at his feet.

The rope was sodden. It took a minute for Max to unravel it. Once more he found the midpoint. He hooked the centre loop over the outcrop and rewrapped it round himself in the Dülfersitz formation. He jumped backwards, praying that the rope would take his weight again.

It did. Max continued his descent.

The mist started to clear so gradually that he didn't notice it at first. But after a couple of minutes, his visibility increased to ten metres, then twenty. The rain was still heavy, but at least he could see around him. He looked over his shoulder, left and right, his eyes narrowed as he scanned the area beneath him.

It was a shock to see how close he was to Jordan. He lay directly beneath Max, on his back on a fairly level part of the slope. He wasn't moving. Max felt momentarily sick.

He kept going. A minute later he was alongside Jordan and unravelling the rope from around his body. The tarn he'd seen from the top of the ridge was about twenty-five metres away, hazy through the elements. He quickly knelt down beside Jordan. Jordan's face was bruised and bloodied. His eyes were closed.

'Be alive,' Max whispered. '*Be alive!*' He felt Jordan's wrist for a pulse. It was weak, but it was there. He put his wet hand up close to Jordan's mouth and nose. He could feel breath. There appeared to be no head wounds or bleeding. Jordan was unconscious, but miraculously alive.

He was also still wearing his rucksack. Max gently rolled him on to one side into the recovery position. It gave him access to the rucksack. He felt inside for the solid brick of the sat phone, praying it wouldn't be damaged. It seemed okay. He powered it on and dialled 999.

'Emergency services.'

Max's voice was raw and hoarse as he shouted, 'Mountain rescue! My name's Max Johnson. I'm on Helvellyn. Striding Edge. It's an emergency! I need mountain rescue! Now!'

The waiting was the worst bit.

Max felt his body temperature dropping. Now that he was standing still, the pounding rain was sucking the heat out of him. He busied himself by attending to Jordan. His pulse was still weak. Max checked it every thirty seconds, ready to perform CPR if it stopped. In the meantime, he tried to keep his patient warm. He rubbed Jordan's hands and fitted his own hat over his head. Then he removed his waterproof jacket and laid it over Jordan. That meant Max would grow colder faster. But Jordan's need was greater.

Max looked around. How would mountain rescue find

them? Max had only managed to give them the sketchiest idea of their position.

He heard it before he saw it. A distant, regular beat of rotary blades. The wind and rain made it difficult to tell which direction it was coming from. But then he saw a kind of shadow in the clouds, descending from the north. He stood up quickly and started to wave his hands above his head. Movement, he knew, was what the helicopter pilot needed to spot him. He shouted as loudly as he could – 'Over here!' – even though he knew he wouldn't be heard.

There was nowhere nearby for the bright orange chopper to land. It hovered about twenty metres above them, buffeted by the high winds. The side door opened and a figure appeared. He wore an orange hard hat and a harness. Attached to a rope, he lowered himself down next to them. 'Is he alive?' he shouted.

'Yes!'

'Good. Help me!' He unclipped himself from the rope and removed a fabric stretcher from his pack. It had straps and several ropes attached to either side. The ends of the ropes were attached to two carabiners, one on each side. 'Get this under him!' he bellowed.

Max helped the rescue guy manoeuvre the stretcher underneath Jordan. Once it was in position, he rolled Jordan on to his back again. The rescue guy strapped Jordan in, then clipped the carabiners to the dangling ropes. He made a thumbs-up sign. Instantly, Jordan was in the air. He swung precariously as he was winched up, but a few seconds later he was safely inside the helicopter.

The rescue guy looked up the slope. 'You abseiled down that?'

Max nodded.

'You're crazy. You could have killed yourself.' He gave Max an uncertain look. 'Where did you learn to do it?'

'A book,' Max said.

The rescue guy shook his head incredulously. But by now the rope had descended again, lashing violently in the wind. The rescue guy grabbed it and clipped it to his harness, then to Max's. 'Hold tight,' he shouted. Max gripped the rescue guy's shoulders and they rose into the air. Seconds later they were being manhandled into the helicopter.

Inside, it was chaotic. A doctor was already treating Jordan. There were three other men in hard hats and harnesses. Max was bundled roughly to the back of the aircraft. He felt their altitude increase. The deafening sound of the engines rose as the chopper moved up towards the top of the ridge. Max knew his work was done. It was down to the professionals now. He felt the chopper bump as it touched down, then watched as Mickey, Suze, Angus and the others were helped or lifted into the chopper. They were all shivering, all pale. And they all looked at Max with an unfamiliar mixture of exhaustion and respect.

Max closed his eyes and breathed deeply. They were still closed when he felt the chopper take to the air again. He was shivering badly, reliving the abseil. The rescue guy was right. He could have killed himself. But he was aware that something else had taken over – a calm steeliness. He knew that if he found himself in that situation again, he'd do exactly the same thing. Not bad for an orphan boy.

It only took a couple of minutes to get back down to safety. Max opened his eyes just as the chopper's landing gear touched the ground. The side door was immediately flung open and he saw the flashing blue neon lights of emergency vehicles. People were barking instructions. Paramedics in high-vis jackets helped everybody who could walk out of the chopper. Mickey and Jordan were carried on stretchers. Max was the last to leave. As he stepped out of the chopper, a paramedic directed him forward, away from the chopper's tail rotors. The main rotors were still spinning and the downdraught was strong. They had landed in an empty car park, cordoned off by police cars. Three ambulances were waiting, and the other climbers were being carried or ushered towards them. Not knowing what else to do, Max followed them.

He had only walked a few steps, his head bowed and shoulders hunched against the downdraught, when he felt a strong hand on his arm.

He heard a voice. Male. Deep, calm and somehow strong enough to be heard above the noise without being raised.

'Not you,' said the voice.

3

Valley House

'What do you mean?' Max said.

'You don't understand two simple words? Perhaps you aren't as smart as they say.'

If the man thought a put-down like that was going to have any effect, he was wrong. Max was used to fighting his corner at school and in the care home.

'No one says I'm smart. What's going on? Who are you?'

Max had never before seen the man who was holding him firmly by the arm. He was only a little taller than Max, but his shoulders were broad. He gave the impression of being immensely strong. It occurred to Max that it would take several men to move him, so there was certainly no point in him struggling. The man wore black jeans, a black polo-neck top and a black waterproof coat. He had a black beard, quite bushy, flecked here and there with grey. His wet wavy black hair blew in the downdraught from the helicopter. His eyebrows were heavy and his tanned forehead lined. If Max had to guess his age, he'd say fifty, but his was the kind of face that could be ten years older or younger. His eyes were dark and penetrating. He had a stare that made Max feel uncomfortable.

'You're coming with me,' he said.

'No way,' Max said. He realised he was slightly scared of this man. 'I'm going with my friends.'

'Friends? From what I heard, you don't have any.'

His words hurt. Max stopped struggling.

'Anyway, let me make this easy for you.' With his free hand the man opened his storm coat to reveal a handgun holstered to his body. 'You're coming with me,' he repeated.

The mountain-rescue guy approached them. He had removed his hard hat and his ginger hair was bedraggled – the rain was still heavy. 'What's going on?' he said.

The man in black flashed an ID card. It seemed to satisfy the mountain-rescue guy, who quickly moved away to attend to the others.

The man in black steered Max away from the helicopter. He looked over his shoulder. The others had congregated around one of the ambulances. Paramedics were handing them blankets, but all their attention was on Max. They stared as the man in black ushered him towards the police vehicles at the entrance to the car park. Two police officers stood there, watching Max sternly. Max didn't understand. Was he in some kind of trouble? But as he and the man in black approached, the policemen stepped aside, allowing them out of the car park. They crossed the road and stood on the edge of a soggy-looking field. The man took a mobile phone from his pocket with his free hand and made a call. 'I've got him,' he said. 'RV in one minute.'

'Where are we going?' Max demanded. 'I need some dry clothes.' He was soaked through.

'Be patient. You sound like a baby.'

'You're a real charmer, you know that?' Max was tired, cold, wet and scared. And he didn't like this guy's attitude. Who did he think he was?

A dark grey shape was descending from the cloud above the field. It was another helicopter but, unlike the mountain-rescue chopper, it had two rotor blades. Max instantly recognised it as a Chinook. He'd lost count of the number of YouTube videos he'd watched of this twin-engine, heavy-lift helicopter transporting military personnel in and out of battle zones in Afghanistan and Iraq. It was the fastest military helicopter, but it looked totally out of place here, in the middle of a sodden field in the Lake District.

'That's our lift,' the man said. He looked down at Max's arm. 'I'm going to let you go,' he said. 'You realise that if you try to run, I'll have you on the ground in about five seconds?'

Max jutted out his chin. But when the man let go, he didn't try to escape.

'Wise move,' the man said. 'Now come with me.'

They approached the Chinook from behind. The tailgate had lowered. The man jogged towards it. Max followed. As they ran into the helicopter, the stench of fuel hit Max's nose. The interior glowed with artificial yellow light. The tailgate clamped shut behind them.

'Sit there.' The man pointed to a bench that ran along the right-hand side of the aircraft. Max dumped his rucksack at his feet and did as he was told. It was very uncomfortable, sitting in his wet clothes.

'Strap yourself in.'

Max looked down at the straps. 'How?'

'What do I look like – cabin crew? Work it out, brainbox.'

It only took a moment to clip himself in. The man sat on a bench directly opposite him. Max felt the Chinook leave the ground. He'd never been in a helicopter before today. Now that momentary sensation of weightlessness was familiar. 'Where are we going?' he shouted over the noise.

But the man had leaned his head against the side of the chopper and closed his eyes. With his serious, lined, craggy face and his dark clothes, he looked like part of the furniture. As if he was more comfortable in the belly of this mechanical beast than anywhere else.

Max realised he was more scared now than he had been on the mountain. Where was he going? Who was he with? The police officers and paramedics hadn't stopped this guy from taking him. But he'd seen a movie once in which the bad guys had been dressed up as police. Was this guy dressed up too?

The man opened his eyes and stared at Max. A slight frown crossed his forehead. It was the expression of a man who thought he recognised someone. 'You abseiled down?' he shouted.

Max nodded.

'What type of abseil?'

'Dülfersitz.'

The man gave a dismissive sneer. 'South African abseil would have been better on a slope that steep.' He closed his eyes again.

'Right,' Max muttered. 'Sorry about that.'

There was no way of knowing in which direction they were flying. He even found it difficult to keep track of the time. Had they been in the air for half an hour? An hour? Longer? His clothes had dried out a little, although his walking boots were still soggy. He was also ravenous. He fished inside his backpack for one of his foil ration packs. The lettering on the side said 'Sausage and Beans' but he'd tried every variety on his CCF field trip and they all tasted the same: awful. He tore it open and squeezed the cold, sludgy food into his mouth. He didn't care that it was disgusting. It was fuel and he needed it.

A wave of tiredness overcame him. His muscles ached, and so did his brain. His eyes felt heavy. He slept.

It was the man in black who woke him, by shaking his

shoulder. Max started violently. For a second he couldn't work out where he was. But then he saw the tailgate of the Chinook lowering. A pale grey light flooded in, hurting Max's eyes after the relative darkness of the Chinook. He could just make out the silhouette of a figure standing at the base of the tailgate.

'Get a move on,' said the man in black. 'We haven't got all day.'

Max unclipped himself and stood up groggily. He followed the man down the tailgate and emerged in yet another wet field. It was many degrees colder, almost freezing. Rain was still falling, but here it was a thick grey sleet that temporarily settled on the ground before melting. Looking around, Max saw that they were surrounded by mountains. Around him there was a collection of single-storey buildings. They had curved roofs made of corrugated iron. Max recognised them as World War II Nissen huts. There were seven in a row. Beyond them stood a large, bleak-looking house of grey stone.

The figure Max had seen at the bottom of the tailgate was a young man. He had sandy hair and an open, honest, ruddy face with smile lines on his cheeks. His nose was wonky – it looked like it had once been broken – but somehow that only made him look friendlier. He was wearing military camouflage gear.

'This him, Hector?' he asked the man in black.

Hector, if that was his name, scowled at the young

man, nodded, and strode off towards the Nissen huts. The young man inclined his head. 'Actually,' he said, 'I didn't think he'd be in such a good mood.'

'Are you kidding?' Max said.

The young man shook his head. 'Oh no,' he said. 'I think he likes you. You're lucky. He doesn't like everybody.' He held out his hand. 'I'm Woody.'

'Right.' Max shook his hand. 'I'm . . . Hang on, can you just tell me what's going on? What am I doing here?' He exhaled heavily. 'It's been kind of a long day.'

Woody looked surprised. 'He didn't tell you why you're here?'

'He didn't tell me anything.'

'Oh.' Woody cocked his head again. 'Maybe he doesn't like you after all. Oh well. Never mind. Come with me.'

Woody strode briskly towards the Nissen huts. More confused than he'd ever been, Max trotted behind him. The peaks of the mountains surrounding them were covered by cloud. To his left, Max saw two more grounded helicopters.

Woody noticed him looking at them. 'They're the only way to get in and out of this valley,' he explained. 'It's inaccessible by road or foot. We're in a remote part of Scotland. Weather's improving,' he added without a hint of sarcasm as they passed the Nissen huts and walked across an area of cracked tarmac.

As they approached the house, Max heard – and

saw – the Chinook pass overhead and head off into the distance. To the left of the secure metal front door, a plaque read 'Valley House'. Woody pressed his finger to a sensor on the right-hand side of the door. It clicked open and they entered. They were in a musty-smelling hallway. Along one wall was a line of black-and-white photographs showing military men and women. Max had little time to examine them, but one of them caught his eye. It was of a young soldier sitting by a small fire in the jungle. It was the soldier's face that caught Max's attention. It looked familiar. It could have been his double, he realised. He felt an uncomfortable sensation in the pit of his stomach, as though he had recognised someone in real life whom he'd long thought to be dead.

'Come on,' Woody called, snapping Max back to reality. He led Max up a staircase, along a dim corridor and into a room filled with sofas and armchairs, shabby but not uncomfortable-looking. Along the far wall was a series of floor-to-ceiling windows framed by thick velvet curtains. Woody walked up to the windows. He turned and made a 'come here' gesture to Max.

Max joined him. He looked out of the window.

The geography of the area immediately became clearer. The house was at the floor of a long valley with steep, rocky mountain slopes on either side. The valley itself disappeared into the sleet haze, but the area behind the house was very clear. It was a puddle-strewn parade ground, populated by thirty or forty teenagers, none of them older than Max. They all wore similar camouflage gear to Woody, and beige berets. They were muddy, bedraggled and obviously exhausted. Some were bent double. Others were on their knees. A couple were retching on the edge of the parade ground.

To one side of the parade ground stood a woman in her twenties. She had fiery red hair pulled into a tight ponytail. She held a wicker basket. Some of the teenagers were queuing up in front of her, their berets in their hands.

Max stared at this peculiar scene for a full thirty seconds without saying anything. Then he turned to his sandy-haired companion with a questioning expression.

'Welcome to the Special Forces Cadets selection camp,' said Woody. 'I've got a feeling you're going to fit right in.'

4

The Watchers

'The what?' Max said.

'The Special Forces Cadets selection camp.' Woody smiled at him again and looked back out of the window. 'Looks like we're losing a few already,' he said.

Max blinked at him. 'Can we just back up a moment?' he said. 'What are the Special Forces Cadets?'

'You know what cadets are, right?'

'Young soldiers.'

'And you know what special forces are?'

'Highly trained soldiers.'

'Well, there you go. Highly trained young soldiers. Couldn't have put it better myself.' Woody frowned. He seemed to be looking at the line of teenagers clutching their berets. One by one they placed them in the wicker basket the young woman held. 'We don't normally lose that many on the first day. Probably the weather.' He turned to Max. His face softened slightly at Max's obvious confusion. 'The Special Forces Cadets are a secret team of young military personnel,' he said. 'Everybody here has been identified as a potential recruit by a team of army scouts. I'm one. Hector's another. We're known as the Watchers. We watch over you, you see.' He pointed at the woman with the wicker basket. 'That's Angel. She's a Watcher too.'

'You've been spying on me?'

Woody looked a little offended. 'Spying is such an ugly word, Max. We've just been taking an interest in you, is all. You tick the boxes.'

'What boxes?'

'Physical. Psychological. We're looking for young people who are fit and strong. Smart people. Determined people. People with endurance and . . .' He hesitated. 'Bravery, I guess. And, of course, we need people that nobody would miss.' He looked out of the window again. 'Most of the kids down there are orphans, or come from backgrounds where not a single person would mind or even notice if they disappeared.'

Max felt a pang of loneliness. He didn't much like that last description, but he had to admit that it did apply to him.

'I guess not many people tick those boxes,' he said quietly.

'Oh, you'd be surprised. We cast our net pretty wide. We look for teenagers all over the world. There's kids down there from South America, Australia, Afghanistan . . . you name it.'

'But how do you find them?'

'I told you,' Woody said, his face suddenly a little more serious. 'We're the Watchers.'

The cadets had all handed Angel their berets. They were trudging, looking dejected, back towards the house.

'There's a four-day selection process,' Woody said. 'Any of the cadets can quit at any time, if they haven't been failed already. They just need to hand Angel their berets. That lot will be heading home first thing in the morning, along with the ones that we decide aren't up to scratch.' He grinned. 'A bit like *X-Factor*. Less singing, of course. And more puking . . .' He frowned at the two kids who were still retching by the parade ground. 'They're not in a good way, are they?'

'How many make it through?' Max asked.

'Only five,' Woody said. 'The Special Forces Cadet team is always a five-person unit. Chances of making it are pretty slim.'

Max shook his head. 'I still don't get it,' he said. 'Why do you even need this team? What can a team of teenagers do that a team of adults can't?'

'You'd be surprised, Max. Young people like you – you're practically invisible.'

'Thanks very much.'

'Don't take it so personally. Imagine you're, I don't know, a terrorist. You'll be on the lookout for military

34

or police personnel. You won't even notice a bunch of kids. In some instances, our cadet teams can get closer to the bad guys than anyone else.'

'Teams? There's more than one?'

'Kids grow up, Max. We have to refresh the personnel every two or three years. That's what's happening today. Valley House needs some new occupants.'

'And what happens to the ones who don't make it? If it's so top-secret, surely they all go back to wherever they've come from and tell everyone where they've been?'

'Oh, sure,' Woody agreed. 'Some of them do. Not many though. I mean, people don't really show off about things they fail at, right? Those who do, tell their friends that they've been to a top-secret training camp in the middle of nowhere to be assessed for an elite group of military personnel. Then their friends laugh at them and tell them not to be so stupid. They don't tend to mention it again after that.'

Max looked out of the window. The remaining cadets were walking away from the parade ground. He assumed they were heading back to the Nissen huts.

'I still don't see where I come in,' Max said. 'There's nothing amazing about me. And I've missed the first day of selection, haven't I?'

Woody nodded slowly. 'I'm not going to lie, Max. It is a weird one. You've been on our radar for a while. No family. Acing all your CCF activities at school. Pretty good brain, by all accounts. You were definitely on my shortlist and I know Angel felt the same. We even went so far as to start concocting a story for the care home about why you had to leave. We were going to tell them you'd been caught robbing an old lady's house and were going to be sent to a young offenders' unit.'

'Thanks.'

'You're welcome! It was Hector who went the full Simon Cowell. Said you weren't up to it. Said you didn't make the grade. Since we all have to agree who gets invited on selection, I'm afraid that meant you were out. But then you went all heroic on us.'

Max was so overwhelmed that for a moment he didn't understand what Woody meant.

'Striding Edge, Max?' Woody prompted.

'Oh,' Max said. 'That.'

'Yeah. That. I heard you abseiled all the way down the northern slope.'

'This guy went over. He had our sat phone.'

'Nice. What abseil did you use?'

'Dülfersitz.'

'Ah. Would have been better to –'

'Yeah, I know,' Max said waspishly. 'South African.'

'Right!' Woody said brightly. 'Listen, we Watchers don't get the last word. We have superiors. When you made that emergency call, it triggered certain alerts. Hector got his instructions to fetch you.'

'They moved pretty fast.'

'That's what we do, Max. We move pretty fast.' Woody wrinkled his misshapen nose. 'This has all happened very quickly for you,' he said. 'We've lifted you out of a world you know and put you into a world you don't. This isn't something you *have* to do. The others were all given the opportunity to pull out before selection started – and some of them did. You have that opportunity too. Why don't you sleep on it? Let us know in the morning if you want to carry on, or if you want to go back home.'

Max looked out of the window again, considering Woody's words. Go back home? To what? Back to the care home, and the school where nobody wanted to be seen in the same corridor as him? Back to having no friends and zero life? No way.

'I'm in,' he said quietly.

'That's what I thought!' Woody said with a grin. 'If you pass, we can teach you the South African abseil in no time at all!' He frowned. 'It's all rather unusual though. I've never seen anyone miss the first day of selection before. Looks like our bosses are happy to make an exception for you.'

'How kind of them,' Max said. The last of the cadets had traipsed dejectedly from the parade ground.

'Too damn kind, if you ask me.' Max and Woody turned to see Hector standing in the doorway. If anything, he looked grumpier than before. 'Sliding down a rock face because some hippy student got the weather wrong isn't the same as passing selection. Being good at CCF isn't the same as what some of these kids have been through. We didn't call you up in the first place because you're not the right fit. There's plenty of kids out there who're smarter and stronger than you. But I don't think we'll need to kick you out. If you don't throw your hat in by the end of day four, I'll eat mine.'

Hector turned and left. The sound of his footsteps faded away as he strode down the corridor.

'You still think he likes me?' Max said.

'That's Hector for you. His bark's worse than his bite. He'll come round.' Woody frowned again. 'Probably. Come on, I'll take you to your hut.'

But Hector had made Max feel a bit uncertain. He didn't move. Instead, he looked anxiously out of the window again.

Woody gave him a steady look. 'You're not really going to say no because some old soldier like Hector gave you a few hard words, are you?'

Max tried to withstand that stare. He couldn't. After a few seconds he lowered his head.

'Thought not,' Woody said brightly. 'Let's get moving. You'll want a decent night's sleep. Tomorrow's going to be . . . well, kind of brutal. You'll enjoy it!'

He walked to the door and left the room. Max felt he had no option but to follow.

5

The Rules

'There are some rules you need to know,' Woody said as they crossed the open ground between the house and the Nissen huts. 'You'll be bunking down with five other boys. You can tell them your first name and they can tell you theirs. But that's it. No background information. Nothing about where you come from or what school you go to.'

'Why?' Max said.

'Because your presence here is a state secret. Most of you will never see each other again, but we can't risk any of you revealing the identities of those cadets who make it through selection. Special Forces Cadets need to work anonymously. Everyone has been told this. They all understand that if they reveal their own personal information, or ask anybody else theirs, they're out of here.'

'How will you know?'

Woody stopped and gave Max another intense look. 'We'll know,' he said. He smiled broadly again and pointed towards one of the Nissen huts. 'Come on, this is yours.'

The hut had a metal door. Woody knocked three times but didn't wait for an answer before entering. Max followed. The inside was spartan. There were three beds along each wall. At the end were two doors: one with a toilet sign, one with a shower sign. Each bed had a locker on one side, and three bare bulbs hung from the ceiling. There was a gentle drumming of sleet on the corrugated iron roof.

Five other boys were in the hut. Each of them was sitting on the edge of their bed, plainly exhausted. Four still wore their muddy camouflage gear. One, a black boy with short dreadlocks, had removed his top. He was muscular. His arms were covered in tattoos. He was chewing gum and, like the other four, stared silently at Max as Woody led him in. There wasn't much friendliness in his stare.

'OK, lads,' Woody announced brightly, 'we've got a new boy. This is Max. Make him feel at home, won't you? Max, why don't you bunk down here next to Lukas?' He indicated the bed next to the black boy. Lukas made no attempt to greet him. He just stared as Max dumped his soggy rucksack on the bed.

'You'll find clean clothes in the locker,' Woody told him. 'Make yourself at home. Dinner in the house in fifteen minutes.'

Woody turned and left the hut.

Max looked around. On the bed next to Lukas was a tall thin boy with floppy blond hair. On the beds along the opposite wall were two thickset boys with brown hair who looked almost as if they could be twins. Next to them was a very slight young man with short black hair, brown eyes and slightly dark skin. He didn't quite look Middle Eastern, but he didn't look British either. He looked a lot less physically strong than the others and his camouflage gear seemed too big for him. There was something about his face, though, that made Max look twice. Although he was young, his eyes seemed older than his years. Max had the impression that he had seen many things, not all of them good.

They were all still staring at him. Max raised an awkward hand. 'Hi,' he said. When nobody replied he added: 'Er, good to meet you.'

'Just stay out of my space,' Lukas said. Max noticed that he had an American accent. Lukas didn't wait for an answer. He lay back on his bed and closed his eyes.

'Right,' Max breathed. 'Thanks for the welcome.' He looked round at the others. The blond boy and the two thickset boys were going about their business. One of them walked to the shower. The others started removing their camouflage jackets. Only the smaller guy was still staring at Max. More than anyone else, he seemed out of place here.

Max turned towards his locker. He saw that the floor between his bed and Lukas's was littered with chewing-gum wrappers. Lukas was chewing gum as he lay on the bed.

Max could smell spearmint. He opened his locker. His camouflage gear was neatly squared away inside. Was now a good time to put it on? He was still in the dirty gear he'd been wearing since morning. He realised he probably didn't smell too fresh. He decided to get changed.

The camo gear was just the right size for him. Rough material, but warm and dry. He folded up his mountain gear and placed it in his locker. When he turned again, he saw that the small guy was standing at the end of his bed. He was still staring at Max. It was kind of freaking him out.

'Er, hi,' Max said.

'Hi,' said the boy.

'I'm Max,' Max said, even though Woody had already introduced him.

'I'm Sami.' Sami had an accent that Max couldn't place. They shook hands. Sami's grip was not very strong.

'Where are you from?' Max asked.

'Hey!' Lukas sat up. 'You know the rules. Names only.'

Max looked around. There were no Watchers to overhear them. 'Sure,' he said. 'I just thought –'

'Don't go ruining this for the rest of us.' Lukas took an empty chewing-gum wrapper from his pocket. He spat his gum into it, wrapped it up and threw it to the floor. He took a fresh piece of gum from his pocket and curled it into his mouth. 'How come you've rocked up a day late, anyway?'

Max gave him a steady look. 'You know the rules,' he said. 'Names only.'

Lukas's lip curled. 'Yeah, well. You won't be staying long. Nor will he.' He pointed at Sami who looked, for a moment, like he might cry.

'He got through the first day, didn't he? That's more than some people did.'

Lukas scowled. 'More than you did too.'

'Yeah, well . . . I've been kind of busy.'

The shower door opened. The thickset boy emerged. Lukas grabbed a towel from his locker and stormed off to the shower.

'He always like that?' Max asked Sami.

'Since yesterday, when we all met,' Sami said quietly. 'He told me this morning that I would never pass.' He bowed his head, a timid gesture, and returned to his bed. It crossed Max's mind that Sami did look very slender. If selection was as difficult as Hector and Woody said, there was probably a chance that he'd struggle.

'What did you have to do today?' Max asked. It was clear to him that the blond boy and the two thickset boys weren't going to talk, so he addressed his question to Sami. 'For selection, I mean.'

'We had to run,' Sami said. 'A long way. Maybe ten miles, without stopping. Then we had to hide in the forest. The ones they found were sent home.'

'Where did you hide?'

'There was a ruined hut. Just a pile of bricks. I clambered in under the bricks.'

'Didn't that hurt?'

Sami gave a small smile. 'I'm used to it,' he said.

'Why?'

Sami gave him a helpless gesture that said, I can't tell you.

Max noticed that the pitter-patter of sleet on the metal roof had stopped. Everything was quiet. Then, somewhere outside, a whistle blew.

'That's dinner,' Sami said. He looked like he was going to invite Max to go with him, but was too shy to do it.

'Shall we go?' Max asked. 'I could do with something to eat.'

Sami smiled and nodded. Together they left the hut.

Just because the sleet had stopped, it didn't mean the weather had improved. The sleet had turned to snow. A blizzard swirled all around them, so thick that the house was a mere outline. Already there was a thin covering of snow on the ground. Max and Sami hurried through it. By the time they reached the house, snow had settled on their hair and clothes. Sami was laughing. His dark, serious eyes twinkled. 'Where I'm from,' he said, 'we never see snow!' He touched the white powder on his clothes like it was magic dust.

'You know what I'm thinking?' Max said.

'What?'

'That whatever they have lined up for us tomorrow, the snow isn't going to help.'

'Oh well.' Sami smiled. 'At least it will be fun!'

Max followed him across the hallway to a large room at the back of the house. There was a school-dinner smell and the sound of voices and clinking cutlery. Inside the room, about twenty cadets were sitting at two long tables. At the far end was a line of hot plates. A woman stood behind them, ready to serve.

'That's Martha,' Sami said. 'She's the matron. She's supposed to look after us.' He gave Max an open, honest look. 'I am extremely scared of her,' he said.

Martha was perhaps sixty years old. She looked severe. She had tanned skin and lines around her eyes and lips. Her wavy hair had blonde highlights and was scraped back in a tight bun, with a couple of tendrils hanging over her forehead. She had her arms crossed and was holding a ladle. It occurred to Max that if she wanted to use it as a weapon, she probably could.

Max and Sami walked up to her in silence. She was standing guard over a cauldron of brown stew. She looked at Max. 'You the new one?' She had a Scottish accent.

Max nodded. Martha looked unimpressed. Wordlessly, she ladled out two bowls of stew and handed them to him and Sami. 'Eat,' she said.

They took their food and walked to the end of one of the long tables. They sat opposite each other. On Max's left was a girl his own age. She had pale skin and blue eyes. Her brown hair was thick, shiny and straight, but dishevelled. She had a double cartilage piercing in her left ear and was very firmly focused on the plate of food in front of her. She didn't even seem to notice Max's arrival.

Max started to eat. The food was bland but hot. He had only swallowed a couple of mouthfuls when the girl next to him spoke.

'I'm Abby,' she said. Her accent was Northern Irish and very strong.

'Hi,' Max said. 'I'm –'

'You going to eat that?'

Max looked down at his bowl of food. 'Er, yeah . . .'

Abby looked across the table at Sami. 'You going to eat that?' she asked.

Sami cradled his food protectively.

'Ah, jeez,' Abby said. 'A girl could starve around here. It's worse than being in prison.'

'How would you know about prison?' Max said.

Abby's eyes tightened slightly. 'What did you say your name was?'

'Max.'

'Well, if you change your mind about that food, Max, you give me a holler.'

She fell silent and sat watching, hawk-like, as they continued to eat their stew. Max ate a bit more quickly. He had the impression she might grab the bowl from him if he didn't hold on to it.

He was halfway through his meal when he saw Lukas.

The American boy held his bowl of stew and stood between the two long tables. He caught Max's eye, then turned his back on him and went to sit by himself at the other table.

'Whoa!' Abby said. 'Awks or what? I guess you really are going to finish that, aren't you?'

'I really am,' said Max.

She stood up. 'I'll see you tomorrow then,' she said. She took her dirty bowl and left.

'She tried to have my breakfast too,' Sami said. He frowned. 'I almost gave it to her. It was something called . . . porridge? I didn't like it much.'

When they had finished their meal they deposited their dirty plates on a trolley by the hotplates and headed out of the dining room. It was only as they were crossing the hallway that Max remembered something. 'Wait a minute,' he said to Sami. He walked up to the line of old photographs he had noticed when Woody first brought him in here, and found the one that had caught his eye: the young soldier sitting by a small fire in the jungle. The soldier looked as if he was staring right at Max. For Max, it was like looking in the mirror. The short brown hair parted on the right. The thick eyebrows and strong jawline. He found himself holding his breath as he stared.

Sami looked from Max to the picture and back again. 'Is that you?' he said.

'Course not,' Max replied. 'It was taken years ago, wasn't it?'

'Looks like you.'

'Yeah, well . . .' Max turned away from the picture. 'Come on,' he said. 'Let's go.'

Outside, the snow was even heavier. It had settled as deep as their ankles and the Nissen huts were covered. Max pulled up the collar of his camo jacket and marched through the snow. He was suddenly overwhelmed with tiredness. It had been a long day.

He was only halfway to the huts when he felt it: a snowball on the side of his head. He looked round to see Sami, bright-eyed and grinning. Max quickly bent down, made a snowball and hurled it at his new friend. It missed by a couple of inches. Sami hooted with glee again, and did a funny little dance that made Max laugh.

'I love snow!' Sami shouted to nobody in particular. He raised his arms up into the air. 'I LOVE SNOW!'

6

White-Out

'I hate snow,' Sami muttered under his breath.

It was 05:30 next day. The remaining recruits – twenty-five of them – were in a straight line on the parade ground. The snow was half a metre thick. The temperature was sub-zero. A biting wind felt like it was freezing Max's bones.

It had been a long, cold night. The Nissen huts were unheated. Max and the others had slept in their clothes underneath their blankets. Even then, their teeth had chattered all night. Hector had woken them at 05:00. with a short, sharp instruction: 'Up. Now!' It was still dark when they trudged through the snow to the house, where they had been given a bowl of porridge and a cup of tea.

And now here they were, standing in the half-light of dawn. Max was colder than he'd ever been. The snow swirled around as thickly as last night, settling on their shoulders and heads. Lukas was on Max's left, chewing gum as always and doing everything he could to ignore Max. He seemed hyped and kept running on the spot to stay warm. Sami was on Max's right, complaining about the snow. Max wondered if his new friend was even listening to Hector.

'Your objective is this,' Hector shouted above the wind as he marched along the line of recruits. 'You are to imagine that there is a hidden weapons cache up in the mountains.' He pointed to his right, at the slope that formed one steep side of the valley. It had looked unforgiving in the sleet. In the snow it looked impassable. 'The cache's position is indicated on a map, which I will give you. You will leave at two-minute intervals and try to locate it. Your objective is marked by a red flag. You will find a fingerprint sensor next to it. When you reach it, scan your fingerprint so we know you have arrived and how long it has taken you. If you do it in the allotted time, you will make it through to day three. If not, you won't. A helicopter will arrive to bring you back down once everyone has checked in at the cache. In the meantime, you'll have to find shelter. You'll each have an emergency distress beacon. If you get lost, or you can't take it any more, activate the beacon by pressing the button. It will send a GPS signal that will allow us to find you. But if you do that, you're out. Any questions?'

Silence. Max glanced along the line of shivering recruits. Nobody looked like they were going to ask a question. He put his hand up. 'How long do we have?'

Hector refused to catch his eye. 'We don't tell you. Do

it as quickly as possible. You'll either pass or fail. Any other questions?'

'When's lunch?'

Max looked to his right along the line and saw that it was Abby who'd asked the question. Hector simply scowled at her. He turned to Woody and Angel, who were standing opposite the recruits. Woody was carrying a pile of maps and compasses in clear protective pouches. Angel had the cigar-shaped distress beacons on lanyards. They walked to the left-hand end of the line and gave a map, compass and beacon to the boy standing there. Hector looked at his watch. 'Go!' he barked.

The first recruit looked bewildered. He looked round at the others, as though expecting some sort of help. But no help came. So he looked instead up at the mountainside that Hector had indicated. He consulted his map, looked up at the mountain for a second time, and then started to run through the snow. He became a grey ghost through the blizzard, then disappeared.

There was a murmur from the line of recruits. Hector was looking at his watch. When two minutes passed, he shouted, 'Next!' Woody and Angel handed out map, compass and beacon, and the second recruit, a girl, hurried off after the first.

Lukas was tenth in line, Max eleventh, Sami twelfth. Once the third recruit had left, Max and Sami started to follow Lukas's lead, jumping up and down to keep warm in the biting cold. Max's hands and feet were already numb. He kept looking at the mountain slope. It was barely visible through the blizzard. How cold would it be up there? He felt a pang of anxiety just thinking about it. And then he thought, I don't have to do it. I can walk away now. Go back to my old life.

But what kind of life was that? He had no home. No friends.

He caught Hector looking at him. As soon as their eyes met, Hector looked away and shouted, 'Next!' Max continued to jog on the spot, determined that he was going to pass this selection.

Twenty minutes after the first recruit had left, it was Lukas's turn. As he waited for Woody and Angel to hand over his map, compass and beacon, he turned to Max. He spat his gum out into the snow and curled a fresh piece into his mouth. 'Don't go following me,' he whispered. It was the first thing he'd said to Max since before dinner the previous night. He had a fiery glint in his eyes. Max could tell he was desperate to succeed.

'I'll be following the map,' Max said.

Lukas scowled at him. Hector shouted, 'Next!' A moment later, map in hand, Lukas had sprinted into the blizzard and disappeared.

Max turned to Sami. His new friend was shivering. Max wondered how he would manage in this cold. 'You've got to keep moving,' Max said. 'That'll keep you warm. If you start to get confused, or sleepy, or your movements are slow, that's hypothermia. If that happens, you have to use the beacon.'

Sami gave him a distressed look.

'But I'm sure that won't happen,' Max added quickly. 'You'll be fine.' Privately, though, Max didn't think he would be. Sami would be going home tonight, wherever home was.

'Next!'

Woody thrust a map and compass into Max's hands and winked at him. Angel hung the lanyard round his neck. Quickly, Max examined the map. A black cross marked their current position. He knew that because the pattern of the contour lines on the map showed that it was in a valley with steep slopes on either side. At the top of the slope was a red flag. That had to be the cache. Max looked at the scale marking on the map and estimated the distance. Three kilometres, uphill. This was going to be tough.

He ran, following the prints left by the recruits who had gone before. There was no sign of any of them up ahead, the visibility was so poor. Looking back after a minute, he couldn't even see Hector, Sami and the others at the starting point.

He stopped for a moment. It was absolutely silent. He looked at the trail of footprints in the snow. They all went off in the same direction. North-west, according to his compass. But as he looked at the map again, he wasn't sure that was the best route. If he was reading it correctly, the path the others were taking followed a ridge to the vicinity of the cache. In this weather, that ridge would be very exposed. Snow could be drifting in the wind, making the route dangerous and inaccessible. And Max felt he'd had enough of dangerous ridges for the time being.

There was another, more sheltered route that would take Max to the south-west – but it was longer than the obvious path. Maybe even half as long again. Should he risk it? Was he crazy? He knew that Hector would jump at any chance to fail him . . .

His gut told him it was the right decision. He headed south-west, through fresh snow. Within twenty seconds, the path the others had followed was out of sight. Max was on his own.

It was a white-out. He couldn't even see the mountain slope up ahead. He checked his compass every ten paces to ensure he was following the correct bearing. After a few minutes, the gradient started to increase. His body temperature rose a little from the extra exertion. He powered through the snow, trying not to worry about his decision. He'd made it now. He had rolled the dice.

Time had little meaning. Max could only focus on the climb. It would have been tough even without the snow. The thick powder on the ground made each step a struggle. His legs hurt and his lungs burned after just twenty minutes. He stopped to look at the map. His route took him up a steep-sided gulley, clearly marked on the map.

He began to panic. He should have stayed with the others. There was safety – and success – in numbers.

It was too late to think like that. The way he saw it, he had only two options: to find the gulley he needed to decide whether to continue on the same trajectory, or change direction and head west.

He consulted his compass and headed west.

The higher he climbed, the deeper the snow got. The blizzard showed no sign of abating. Max stopped regularly to check his direction and to look at his surroundings. But the visibility was so poor that, really, he could be anywhere.

He tried to gauge how high he had climbed. Maybe one hundred and fifty metres? He checked the map again. The cache was at three hundred and sixty-five metres. He wasn't even halfway there.

He pushed on. The temperature was dropping, the snow becoming icier and more slippery. Several times he stumbled and fell. Half an hour passed. An hour. Maybe longer. He tripped. His left ankle twisted and he called out in pain. His voice echoed. He hoped nobody had heard.

He winced. He wasn't sure he could get up. All the energy seemed to have drained from his body. He was tired. Sleepy, almost. He wondered if he should just lie down for a while. Get some kip. Carry on when he had more energy . . .

No! A voice rang in his head. What had he told Sami? *If you start to get confused, or sleepy, or your movements are slow, that's hypothermia. If that happens, you have to use the beacon.*

He shook himself awake. The beacon was there, hanging round his neck. All he had to do was press the button and someone would come to rescue him. Slowly his hands crept towards it.

Then they stopped. He pictured Hector standing over him with an 'I told you so' look on his face.

Max grimaced at the thought. He would have to be in a far worse position for *that* to happen. He pushed himself painfully to his feet.

He blinked heavily. Something had just occurred to him. When he had fallen and shouted out, his voice had echoed.

But what had it echoed against?

He shouted out again. 'Hello! *Hello!*'

His voice returned to him a fraction of a second later. The echo seemed to come from his right. He staggered in that direction. Suddenly, through the blizzard, a high vertical wall of rock came into view.

Max grinned. All his sluggishness had fallen away. He checked the map again and pinpointed the two walls of rock that marked his ascent. He was on the right track.

He headed uphill. The cold air was sharp against his face, but he had renewed energy as he battled through the blizzard. Ten minutes passed. Twenty minutes. The steep slope levelled off. Max stood to catch his breath. He had been so intent on climbing that he hadn't realised that it wasn't snowing so hard up here. As he looked around, he could see swirls of cloud. His surroundings appeared for a few seconds, then disappeared again, enshrouded in mist. It cleared again – and Max saw that he was not alone.

The ridge line that he expected the others would be following was about fifty metres to his right. There was nobody on it. Max reckoned he'd made the right call: that route was too slow. But between him and the ridge line, cutting up through another snow-filled gulley, was a figure striding up the hill. Max only glimpsed the figure for a few seconds but he was certain that he recognised the form and the gait.

It was Lukas. He stopped and looked directly at Max. Then the mist swirled between them again. They were hidden from each other.

Max had never thought of himself as competitive. That had changed. He felt a powerful urge to beat Lukas. He checked his map and took a moment to orientate himself properly. He estimated that the cache was 250 metres north-west of his position. Although he and Lukas were approaching it from different angles, they had a similar distance to travel. It would all come down to speed.

Max surged forward. His ankle hurt and he tripped a couple of times as he pushed himself through the snow, and he cursed under his breath. But he kept moving. The mist cleared again and he caught sight of Lukas. His opponent was no faster than him, but he was certainly no slower. They were neck and neck.

His muscles ached. His lungs burned. Through a gap in the swirling mist he could see, up ahead, a red flag stuck in a snow mound. It was twenty, maybe thirty, metres away. As he advanced on the target, all he could hear was his breath and his fast-pumping heart. He could sense Lukas to his right, even though he couldn't see him.

And then he could. He was five metres away, his head down, his face fierce. They raced up the snowy knoll to the flag. As they approached, they shoulder-barged each other. Neither boy was thrown off-course, however. They fell on the flag at precisely the same time, tumbling to the ground as they did so.

Max lay in the snow, catching his breath. Lukas stood up immediately, brushing himself down and muttering angrily under his breath. To the right of the flag was a post. The fingerprint sensor was attached to it. Lukas pressed his thumb to the screen and nodded in satisfaction. Max stood up too. He felt a little embarrassed by his sudden competitiveness. They were supposed to be racing an unknown time limit, not each other. He pressed his thumb to the sensor. A neon-green light scanned it.

'So what kept you?'

Max blinked. It wasn't Lukas who had asked the question. It was someone on the far side of the snowy mound. A female voice with an Irish accent. He and Lukas exchanged a look, then peered over the leeward side of the mound. Abby was sitting there. She looked quite comfortable, sitting cross-legged and eating a chocolate bar. She gave them a friendly little wave.

Max stared at her. He looked over his shoulder, then back at Abby. 'You left after us,' he said.

'You're a sharp one,' she said. 'Max, wasn't it?'

'But how did you get here so quickly?' Lukas said

Abby put one finger to her lips, pretending to think hard. 'Well, Lukas my friend, I guess that would be by moving faster.'

'Where's everyone else?' Max asked, looking around.

Abby shrugged and took another mouthful of her chocolate bar. 'I passed a few on the way,' she said.

Max became aware of movement behind him. Lukas was stalking off, apparently furious that he hadn't been first. Beyond him, heading up the ridge, were two figures side by side. One of them was obviously injured. The other was helping the casualty up the slope. They were momentarily obscured by the mist. When they came back into view, Max saw that it was Sami helping the injured person towards the flag. Max sprinted towards them.

Sami was sweating hard despite the cold. The injured person was the blond boy from their sleeping quarters. He had one arm over Sami's shoulder and only seemed to be able to use his right leg. His left was bent backwards at the knee. He looked like he'd broken a bone. His face was white with cold and pain.

'What happened?' Max shouted as he took the blond boy's other arm around his shoulder.

'I found him. He had tripped on a hidden rock. He fell on his beacon and it broke. I offered to use mine but he wouldn't let me. I thought it would be better to get him to the top where we can help him together.'

The blond boy was too cold and in too much pain to talk. Max wondered what state he would have been in if Sami had just left him.

They reached the flag with difficulty. Abby and Lukas were waiting for them. Abby looked mildly bemused. Lukas was frowning. The blond boy collapsed. 'He needs to get down,' Max shouted. 'He needs medical care.'

Sami nodded. Abby inclined her head as though listening. Lukas scowled.

'We should all activate our beacons,' Max told them. 'That way they'll know there's a real emergency.'

Sami immediately held up his own beacon. Abby and Lukas hesitated. Max pointed at the casualty. 'He could die,' he shouted. 'Is all this so important to you that you're willing to let that happen?'

60

Abby and Lukas looked at each other. Then they held up their beacons.

'If we get sent home because of this . . .' Lukas snarled.

'Just do it!' Max shouted. 'Three, two, one . . .'

The four teenagers activated their beacons together.

When the helicopter arrived, piloted by Angel, it was the most dangerous thing Max had ever seen. The snow was still falling, the mist still swirling. Visibility was poor – barely twenty metres. To fly in those conditions, almost blind, took a skill and strength of nerve few people had. As the chopper touched down on the mountaintop, the downdraught from the rotors blew up a huge cloud of snow that almost completely obscured the helicopter itself. Seconds later, Hector and Woody emerged from the snow cloud and sprinted towards them.

By now, a few other recruits had arrived. They had pressed their thumbs to the fingerprint sensor and were standing around, trying to keep warm and looking anxiously at the blond boy, who was lying shivering in the snow. Hector and Woody strode through them and took one look at the casualty. They nodded at each other, then picked him up with one arm round each shoulder. 'Get in the helicopter, everybody!' Hector shouted as they carried the blond boy to the chopper.

The recruits looked at each other. Then they ran through

the swirling cloud of snow, which harshly bit the skin on their faces, to the aircraft.

Over the thunder of the rotor blades, Max could just hear Hector's voice shouting, almost screaming: 'Whoever activated their beacons, you're going home. Tonight!'

7

R.E.J.

In the chopper, all was confusion. Hector bellowed at the recruits to sit down and shut up while he and Woody tended to the casualty. The recruits looked on, silent and anxious. Max couldn't see what the Watchers were doing to the blond boy because Woody, hunched down over him, was in the way. All he knew was that it was serious, urgent and best left to them. As the chopper was buffeted on its way back down the mountain, he found he could concentrate on only one thing: Hector's words ringing in his head. *You're going home.*

The chopper touched back down on the valley floor. Hector and Woody carried the casualty off the aircraft. Martha, the matron, was waiting for them. She had her arms folded and a pitiless look on her face. She pointed at the house and the two Watchers carried their casualty towards it. The others disembarked. Max, Sami, Lukas and Abby were in stunned silence. Lukas stormed away as soon as they were on the ground. It almost felt as if his anger would melt the snow.

It was only when Woody returned and was approached by Abby and Sami that the Watchers learned the truth about what had happened. Max watched them and felt Hector's hot glare across the parade ground. He saw Woody turn to the older man and talk fast. Hector threw his hands up in the air and strode back into the house. Woody approached Max. 'Sounds like you have a knack for mountain rescue,' he said.

'It was Sami, really,' Max said.

'Well, ignore what Hector said. He spoke too soon, and in the heat of the moment. You're both through. Lukas and Abby too.' Woody looked across the parade ground to where seven recruits had lined up, caps in hand. 'Another high dropout rate today,' he observed.

It was even higher than Woody thought. At dinner that night, only eight recruits remained. They were silent as they queued up at the hotplate. Martha ladled out bowls of a slightly different-coloured stew and they ate it wordlessly at the long table. Even Abby was quiet. Having eaten her own meal, she glanced hungrily at the others' bowls. But she didn't ask if anyone was going to eat theirs. After a day in the mountains, they were all hungry.

That night, Max dreamed of rocky ridges, cloud lines and snow. He woke up several times, sweating. It had been a brutal forty-eight hours. His muscles hurt, but so did his mind. As he lay in the darkness, he realised that the Watchers weren't only testing their physical endurance;

they were also testing them mentally. Maybe that was why Hector was being so aggressive with Max. But then why wasn't he acting like that with the others?

When morning arrived, Max heard the sound of rain on the iron roof of the Nissen hut. It was heavy and persistent. When he stepped outside just before dawn, he saw that the snow had mostly melted and a dank drizzle filled the valley. He wondered if the sun ever shone here.

The others were still asleep and there was no sign of the Watchers. Max jogged through the drizzle to the main house and was a little surprised to find the front door open. He stepped inside and quietly closed the door. He wasn't quite sure what he was doing. But then he found himself walking up to the picture of the young man who looked so very like him. He realised that he'd been intending to look at it again ever since he'd climbed silently out of bed.

It was dark in the corridor where the picture hung. But the young man's face was clearly visible. The first time Max had seen it, he'd been freaked out. Now he found it calming. Looking at it gave him the strength to face whatever the day ahead might throw at him.

He heard footsteps. They were upstairs, but he could tell they were approaching the staircase. They were brisk and firm. It sounded like Hector. And he knew he didn't want to be caught here, even though he wasn't sure whether he was breaking any rules. He tiptoed up the corridor and stepped into a room on his left. There he stood with his back to the wall, holding his breath. The footsteps grew louder. They walked past the room in the direction of the main door. Max heard their owner exiting the house. He exhaled slowly and only then did he look around the room.

It was dark and musty. Heavy curtains covered the windows, but they let a few beams of grey dawn light into the room. It was oak panelled, and there were lots of big, squashy sofas and armchairs dotted around. There was a large fireplace with a substantial store of wood to one side. Above the fireplace was an oil painting. Max couldn't take his eyes off it. It showed a man in full military dress. He had short brown hair, parted on the right. Thick eyebrows. A strong jaw. He looked calm and in control. He also looked exactly like the man in the photo in the corridor. Which meant he looked exactly like Max.

Max stared up at the painting in the gloomy light. He found he was holding his breath again. The picture had an ornate gilt frame. On the bottom edge was an oval panel. Etched on the panel, in fussy copperplate writing, were the letters 'R.E.J.'

'R.E.J.,' Max whispered to himself. 'Who are you?'

'What the *hell* do you think you're doing in here?'

Max spun round to see Hector standing in the doorway. He hadn't heard him come in. Hector looked furious. He glared at Max, then up at the picture, then at Max again. 'I said, what the hell do you think you're doing in here?'

'Exploring,' Max said calmly. He pointed up at the picture. 'Who's that?'

'What does it matter?'

'I was just curious.'

'He's some old soldier. How would I know who it is? What am I, a museum curator?'

It was very faint, but Max saw it: a twitch on the right-hand side of Hector's face as he spoke. He knew the older man was lying. Max also knew he had zero chance of getting the truth out of him.

'Get out of here,' Hector said. 'Breakfast.' He stood to one side of the door and pointed back out into the corridor.

Max avoided Hector's eye as he left the room. He walked along the corridor, across the hallway and into the room where they took their meals. None of the other cadets had arrived yet, but Martha was there. She was fiercely brandishing her ladle behind the hotplate as usual. She glared at Max as he approached.

'What happened to him?' Max asked.

'To whom?' Martha asked sourly in her strong Scottish accent.

'The guy who broke his leg?'

'He cried. A lot.'

'Did you fix him?'

'What do you think this is, laddie? Hogwarts? You think I can wave a magic wand and cure a broken bone? He's in hospital, of course.'

'How long will he be there for?'

'That's none of your business.'

'I helped get him down, didn't I?'

'What do you want?' Martha asked. 'A twelve-gun salute? You've come to the wrong place, laddie, if that's the case.'

'I thought you were here to look after the recruits,' Max said.

'Aye, but not mollycoddle them. If you want someone to mop your fevered brow, you should throw your hat in right now.' She narrowed her eyes. 'It wouldn't be a bad thing anyway.'

Something snapped in Max. He was sick of this attitude, first from Hector and now from Martha. 'Why?' he demanded. 'Why have you brought me here if all you're going to do is put me down?'

Martha stared at him. For the briefest moment, he thought her face might have softened. But it hardened again as she ladled out a bowlful of grey slop. 'Eat your porridge, laddie,' she said quietly. It was clear that the conversation was at an end. Sullenly, he took his breakfast and sat alone at one of the long tables to eat it.

The others arrived one by one: Sami first, then Abby, then Lukas. The two thickset boys from their hut had handed in their caps the previous day. The blond boy was of course no longer with them. There were two other boys who introduced themselves as Jack and Ash. Jack had a shaved head and a tattoo on the back of his left hand. He seemed kind of arrogant to Max. Ash had curly brown hair and a stud in his left ear. Abby introduced two more girls. Their names were Maddy and Els and they didn't speak.

All the recruits looked exhausted. The previous day's exertions had clearly taken it out of them. As Max finished his porridge in silence, he looked from one to the other. He wondered what the day held, and how many of them would be sitting here at supper time.

He was about to stand up when Angel walked in. Max hadn't spoken to her yet. He felt slightly nervous of the tall, silent young woman with the fiery red hair. She seemed neither as aggressive as Hector nor as friendly as Woody. Somehow that made Max respect her all the more. The cool way she had manoeuvred the helicopter on the mountain suggested she was not someone to mess with. Max had the impression that the others felt the same. Even Lukas looked at her with something approaching admiration. She stood at the end of the long table where they were all eating breakfast and looked at each one of them in turn.

'You did well yesterday,' she said in a husky voice. 'All of you. If any of you are thinking of handing in your berets at the end of today, you shouldn't.'

She looked at them all in turn again. Was it Max's

imagination, or did she stare at him for just a fraction longer than the others?

'Line up outside in ten minutes,' she said abruptly. She turned on her heel and strode towards the door. 'Today's exercise: weapons.'

8

Semi-Automatic

There was an excited buzz among the recruits. Whether it was the prospect of weapons handling, or the idea of not having to fight through howling blizzards, Max wasn't sure. But even he had to admit that he felt a little more energised as he filed out of the house with the others. Sami was by his side. 'I've done a bit of weapons handling in CCF,' Max whispered to his friend. 'I'll give you some tips, if you like.'

Sami smiled at him. 'Maybe,' he said.

The rain had lifted. Angel, Hector and Woody were waiting for them outside. They led the recruits round to the parade ground and along the valley for about five minutes. They reached a low concrete building, securely padlocked. Beyond it was a shooting range. At one end was a row of sandbags. Fifty metres further on there was a line of eight targets, each in the shape of a human body. Behind the targets, a solid wall of more sandbags. Max assumed this was to stop any stray bullets travelling too far.

Woody unlocked the building. He, Angel and Hector disappeared inside. The recruits waited. There was a hush. Max found himself standing next to Lukas. He was chewing gum, as usual. When he caught Max's eye, he spat his gum out into a wrapper and threw it on the ground. He was putting a fresh piece in his mouth as the Watchers exited the building. They were carrying weapons. Each of them had a different kind. Woody had the smallest, Angel the next largest and Hector the biggest.

Hector stepped forward. He scanned the recruits standing in front of him. 'Don't get too excited,' he barked at them. 'Special Forces Cadets will seldom be sent into operational situations carrying weapons. We're not raising a pack of gun-hungry teenagers. But the cadets who make it through selection will find themselves in scenarios where the bad guys are armed. You need to show us that you have the potential to learn about the weapons you may encounter. At the end of the day you will each be tested on what you have learned. We are also going to be firing some weapons. This will test certain characteristics that we are looking for: strength, coordination, ability to learn. Maybe you think today will be easier than previous days. Think again. Gun work is all in the head. If your head's not up to it, you're going home.'

He turned to Woody and nodded. Woody stepped forward and held up his firearm. 'This is a handgun, or pistol,' he announced. 'A SIG Sauer P226, to be precise.

It fires 9mm rounds. It's a semi-automatic. I'm now going to explain to you what that means.'

Lukas made a huffing sound and rolled his eyes, as if he already knew everything Woody was going to tell them. Max turned his attention back to Woody.

'Semi-automatic means that once a round is fired, the recoil ejects the empty cartridge case, loads the next round and cocks the weapon. This means the user only needs to cock it once, for the first shot. After that, they are able to fire the remaining rounds in quick succession. All shots today will be discharged in semi-automatic mode. Semi-automatic pistols have advantages and disadvantages. They are easy to conceal and can usually fire twelve or thirteen rounds in quick succession. But they have many working parts, which means they are prone to stoppages. In the movies, you see people accurately firing handguns across large distances. It's not like that in real life. These weapons are hard to aim. A highly competent weapons handler could aim a shot at twelve to fifteen metres. An inexperienced shooter is unlikely to be on target above three to five metres. Those of you who make it through selection will learn how to load and strip down all these weapons. And how to fire them, of course.'

Woody stepped back. Angel took a step forward. She held up her weapon. 'MP5 submachine gun,' she announced. Even Lukas was paying attention now. 'Submachine guns offer the user the portability of a handgun with the firepower of a machine gun. They are generally designed to use the same ammunition as a pistol, but in larger quantities and at a higher rate of fire. We're talking twenty- to thirty-round magazines. The range of a submachine gun is much higher than that of a pistol. A skilled user can get a shot on target at about sixty metres. The rounds themselves will travel for a good hundred and twenty metres. Like the handgun, this weapon can be set to semi-automatic. However, it also has a fully automatic function. On this setting, the weapon will continue to fire bursts of rounds so long as the trigger is pressed and there is enough ammunition in the magazine. For this reason, submachine guns are often used by gangs firing randomly in drive-by shootings. It's called spray and pray.'

For a fraction of a second, Angel glanced at Lukas. Lukas looked at the ground. Then the moment passed. Hector stood forward with his firearm, the largest of the three. He looked very comfortable with it slung across his chest. Max could tell he was well used to carrying such a weapon. It suited him.

'M16 automatic assault rifle,' he stated. 'Magazine fed. Longer barrel. Higher calibre rounds such as 7.62 and 5.56. You see a bad guy with one of these? Run. An untrained operator will likely hit a target with an assult rifle at three hundred metres. A trained operator at six hundred metres. And they're deadly far beyond that.

These are intended as weapons of war, but terrorists and militants all over the world are in possession of them. Assault rifles like this can penetrate glass and steel, so you can guess what they do to humans. If any of you are still under the impression that firearms like this are fun toys, say now and I'll tell you about the men and women I've known who have been killed by them.' He looked at each of them in turn, his characteristic scowl etched deep on his face. The recruits looked back at him in silence.

'Right!' Woody said eagerly. 'Let's get to the range, shall we?'

Max could tell that the group was now more nervous than excited. They lined up by the sandbags while the Watchers disappeared back into the building. When they reappeared, Woody was still carrying the handgun. Angel and Hector were carrying boxes. Max assumed these contained ammunition. Hector looked along the line of recruits. He selected Abby. 'You, come with us. The rest of you, wait here.'

Abby stepped forward, eyes darting from side to side as she tried to judge the reaction of the other recruits. Hector was already striding down the range towards the targets. Woody gave Abby an encouraging smile. 'Come on,' he said.

'Let's show these guys how it's done,' Angel added.

Abby followed them hesitantly down the range. The remaining recruits watched silently. Abby and the others stopped at the far end of the range, ten metres from the nearest target. The Watchers stood around her. They seemed to be showing her how to load and unload the handgun. How to hold it. How to aim it.

And finally, how to fire it.

Her arm was outstretched. The weapon was in her right hand, and steadied by her left. She released three rounds, then made the weapon safe, then handed it back to Woody. Max had to squint to see how accurate her shots were. Two were just outside the outline of a body printed on the target. One was just above the heart. Was that good? He didn't know. Abby didn't seem pleased. She trudged back to the others, head bowed. She looked at Ash. 'They want you,' she said, before sitting on a sandbag a little way from the others.

Ash fared slightly better than Abby, Jack slightly worse. Neither Maddy nor Els were on target. Lukas went next. He was astonishingly good. He held the firearm one-handed and released three rounds in quick succession. The bullet holes were closely clustered around the target's heart. He handed back the gun and returned to the others. If he was pleased with his performance, he didn't show it. 'You,' he said to Sami as he took a seat on a sandbag and stared resolutely back down the range.

Sami gave Max a 'wish me luck' look. Max felt for his new friend. He looked so diffident walking down the range. Unlike Lukas, he listened patiently to the Watchers, nodding in all the right places. When his time came to fire at the targets, he looked unsure as he raised the gun in his right hand and supported it with his left. He fired three shots, then lowered his gun and handed it back to Woody.

There was one bullet hole, directly in the centre of the target's chest. At first Max thought that the other two rounds had missed the target entirely. But the Watchers were looking at each other in astonishment. Max realised that all three of Sami's rounds had hit exactly the same spot. Sami handed over his weapon and walked back up the range. Max expected to see a small smile of achievement on his face. But there was none. If anything, his friend looked distraught. He was on the verge of tears.

'What's up, buddy?'

But Sami just shook his head and said, 'You're next.'

Max was confused, but the Watchers were looking in his direction. He didn't want to keep them waiting so he jogged down the range to meet them. He was the last recruit to fire the handgun. He knew he couldn't beat Sami or Lukas. He would just have to do his best.

He listened carefully as Woody explained in more detail about safety catches and loading mechanisms. 'Keep your finger outside the trigger guard,' he said. 'When the time comes to fire, don't yank at the trigger. Squeeze it, hold it, then gently release. Breathe regularly. Don't hold your breath too much or you'll start to shake.' He handed Max the pistol. 'Good luck,' he said.

'He'll need it,' Hector growled.

'Hey, big guy,' Angel said. 'Go easy on the kid.'

But Hector's words were like a worm in Max's brain. As he stepped up to the firing point and cocked the weapon like he'd been shown, he realised his hand was shaking. He tried to steady it by taking some slow, shallow breaths as he raised his weapon and aimed at the target.

He took a shot. He saw that it had landed wide of the body target, and felt sick. He could almost feel Hector's hot glare on him, and sense his smugness. Somehow it just made him more determined. He steadied his breath again. Took a second shot.

Better. Nothing as close to the chest as Lukas or Sami had managed, but only a few centimetres to the left. 'Sweet,' he heard Angel say. There was of course no word of encouragement from Hector.

He lined himself up for the third shot. Calmed himself. Fired.

It was a perfect shot. As accurate as Sami's, straight through the centre of the target's chest. Knowing that Hector would be watching his every move, he moved his finger to the outside of his trigger guard. Then he handed the weapon back to Woody. He was aware of Hector glowering at him, and he was tired of it. He knew better than to challenge him, however. Instead, he turned to Woody. 'Thanks for the lesson,' he said mildly, and walked back up the range to the others.

The handgun lesson had taken over an hour. The submachine gun lesson took longer. There was more to learn, and the safety procedures were more involved. Again they approached the targets individually, this time standing fifty metres away. It became gradually apparent that the recruits' aptitude, or lack of it, with the pistol had been no fluke. When it came to firing the MP5, Abby and Ash were passable. Maddy, Els and Jack struggled. Lukas looked like he'd been handling one of these weapons all his life. Sami's skill was offset by the tears that threatened to roll down his cheeks at the sound of gunfire. Max himself showed little initial brilliance, but learned quickly. Hector seemed to find this galling, but kept his comments to himself.

After lunch, they tackled the assault rifle. Even Lukas found this beast of a weapon difficult to handle. The kickback bruised Max's shoulder and the retort of the single shots numbed his ears. He only landed one shot on target. Sami, however, was as accurate as ever. His three shots landed right on top of each other. The Watchers were clearly astonished at how good he was. Sami was just as clearly in no mood to accept their admiration. Now his tears flowed freely, and he avoided the others as he walked back up the range. Max didn't know why he was upset, but he couldn't help wondering how he would react if he was ever in a real combat situation.

It was mid-afternoon by the time the weapons-handling

exercise was over. The Watchers locked the firearms in the store and led the recruits back up to the parade ground. The sun was trying to shine. There was even a bit of warmth on Max's back as they lined up at Hector's instruction.

'Does anybody want to throw in their hat?' he asked.

Max looked along the line. Lukas was jutting his chin out defiantly. Abby looked uncertain, but stayed put. It was Sami, standing next to Max, who appeared tempted. It was clear to everyone that he was the best weapons handler and the sharpest shooter. But he seemed on the brink of stepping forward. Max put one hand on his shoulder. Sami gave him a grateful look and kept his place.

When it became clear that nobody was putting themselves forward, Hector nodded. 'In that case,' he said, 'the people going home tonight are . . .'

He caught Max's eye. Max felt sure his name was about to be called. He felt his stomach turn.

'. . . Maddy and Els. Get your kit, girls. The chopper will be ready in half an hour.'

Woody looked sympathetically at them. Angel frowned. Max sensed that she didn't like the idea of the two girls being sent home. The girls hung their heads and started to walk back to the Nissen huts. Woody and Hector followed, then the remaining recruits: Sami, Lukas, Abby, Jack and Ash. All except Max, who hung back to talk to

Angel. He was still slightly in awe of her, a little nervous maybe. But he felt that, out of any of the Watchers, she was the most likely to give him a straight answer.

'Lukas and Sami have used weapons like that before, right?'

'You know the rules,' Angel said curtly.

'I just thought you could tell me –'

'You thought wrong.'

Angel started to follow the others. Max kept up with her.

'You looked at Lukas when you talked about drive-by shootings. Is that what he's into? Gang stuff? I've seen his tattoos.'

Angel looked straight ahead and didn't reply.

'What about Sami? How come he's such a crack shot with an assault rifle? Why does it make him cry?'

'Seriously, Max, you ask me another question like that and you're on the next chopper out of here.'

She upped her pace. Max stopped. 'Hey, Angel,' he called after her, 'who's R.E.J.?'

Angel stopped abruptly. Max saw her shoulders rise as she inhaled deeply. She turned and looked Max directly in the eye.

'I don't know what you're talking about,' she said. She held his gaze for a full five seconds. Then she turned her back on him and continued on her way.

As Max watched her go, he wondered if the Special

Forces Cadets training would include learning to tell if somebody was lying. Not that he needed special training in this instance, because Angel was obviously not telling the truth.

9

Paracord

It was the final day of selection and there were six recruits left: Max, Lukas, Sami, Abby, Jack and Ash. Woody had made it clear that only five people would pass selection. At the end of today, one of them was going home.

They were all nervous. Max could tell. Even Sami and Abby, normally so chatty, were subdued and silent as they sat at breakfast. Martha watched over them sternly. Max had muscle pain from yesterday's shooting, but there was no way he would mention that to the severe matron. He knew what was good for him.

They filed quietly out of the house and on to the parade ground, where the Watchers were waiting for them. The sky was blue. Though some snow remained on the mountain slopes to either side, conditions had markedly improved. A white minibus was parked up on the parade ground. Six rucksacks were lined up in front of it. Next to each rucksack was an M16 assault rifle, identical to the one they had fired the previous day. The rucksacks looked heavy.

They *were* heavy. Before speaking, Hector lifted one. He was a strong guy, but he clearly didn't find the rucksack easy to lift. He dropped it. It landed solidly on the ground with a thump.

'You each have a twenty-five-kilogram pack,' he announced. 'They're filled with gear that a soldier might be expected to carry with them in the field – medical packs, rations, ammunition boxes, dry clothes, paracord.'

Sami put up his hand. Hector looked frustrated. 'You're not at school, Sami. What is it?'

'Please, what is paracord?'

'Light nylon rope, used for suspension lines in parachutes. Very useful in the field. When I tell you, you will strap your pack to your back. You're free to take it off at any time, but if you do, you've failed selection.' He gave each of them a harsh look. 'You will also all carry a rifle. These are unloaded, so no funny business.' Hector's gaze fell momentarily on Lukas as he said this. 'The march is fifteen kilometres. Its route takes you along the valley floor, past the range, through an area of dense forest.' He looked over his shoulder at the minibus. 'Angel and I will skirt around the forest to get to the finish line quickly, but you are not allowed to. Remember, this is not a navigation exercise. Your way will be marked by flags. All that matters is speed and endurance. You will leave at ten-minute intervals. The slowest recruit will leave us tonight. The remainder will be badged as Special Forces Cadets. Are there any questions?'

Hector didn't look like he really wanted to field questions from anybody. There were none.

'Angel and I will set off now for the finish line. Woody will give you your marching orders.'

Hector turned his back on them and climbed behind the wheel of the minibus. Angel hesitated. 'Good luck, everyone,' she said, before getting into the passenger seat.

They waited ten minutes. The minibus was out of sight when Woody turned to them all. He seemed to be trying to decide who should be the first to leave. Eventually his eyes landed on Sami. 'You first, mate,' he said. 'Let's get you sorted.'

He led Sami to one of the packs and helped him put it on. He slung the weapon across Sami's chest. Sami looked like he might collapse under the weight.

'You okay, buddy?' Woody asked.

Sami nodded unconvincingly.

'Then go.' Woody gave him an encouraging slap on the shoulder. Sami glanced at the others, gave Max a quick smile, then ran.

It took five minutes for Sami to disappear from view. Meanwhile, Woody selected Ash and told him to prepare himself. By the time ten minutes were up, Ash was loaded down and ready to go. He followed Sami at a decent pace.

Abby went next. She was obviously stronger than she looked. The weight of the rucksack didn't seem to bother her as much as it had the others. When Woody announced that Jack would be next, Lukas hissed slightly between his teeth. It was clear that he didn't want to be left alone with Max. Max saw Jack wince a little as he put on the rucksack. When Woody asked him if he was okay, he brushed the Watcher away with a curt, 'I'm fine.' They could all see, however, that he was limping a little as he followed Abby, who had disappeared after a few minutes.

Woody turned to them. Max was crouching, watching Jack go. Lukas had his back turned to them. 'You two,' Woody said, 'I want a word.'

Lukas turned slowly. Max stood up. There was something in Woody's voice. Until now, he had been chirpy and encouraging. Now he sounded deadly serious. 'You think this is a game?' he said.

Silence.

'I said, do you think this is a game?'

'No,' they said in unison.

'What do you think is the most important quality in a Special Forces Cadet?' he asked. 'Fitness? Endurance? Sharp shooting?'

Lukas shrugged.

Max said, 'I don't know.'

'Then I'll tell you. It's the ability to look out for your mates. We're not messing around here. The five recruits who make it through today will be put into situations of unimaginable danger. If they're unable to work as a team, their operations will probably fail and they'll likely die.'

Silence.

Woody looked from one to the other. 'Do you think you can work as a team? Well, do you?'

'Yeah,' Max said. 'I think so.'

Lukas nodded. But he failed to look either of them in the eye. Woody surveyed them both. He didn't look as if he believed them. 'Lukas,' he said, 'you're next. Let's get you prepped.'

Lukas didn't want any help putting on the rucksack, or slinging the weapon across his chest. He loaded up and faced in the direction of the course without speaking to or even looking at Woody or Max. When Woody gave him the go-ahead, he sprinted. And of course he didn't look back.

'Lukas is going to make it, isn't he?' Max said. 'He's going to be a cadet.'

'Hector likes him,' Woody said. 'And the people above Hector, they like him too.'

'Why doesn't Hector like me?'

'He does,' Woody said. He made an obvious effort to become his former chirpy self. 'Course he does. Come on, let's get you ready.'

The rucksack was even heavier than it looked. In a way, Max was glad of the M16's weight. He felt more balanced with it slung across his front. But the combined weight felt like it was pulling him down to earth. Woody stood in front of him. 'Pace yourself,

Max,' he said. It was the first time he'd given any advice. 'Don't use too much energy too soon. Now go. Knock it out of the park.'

Max ran. There was no sign of Lukas. With Woody's advice ringing in his ears, he suppressed his urge to sprint. Keep a steady pace, he told himself. Think tortoise and hare.

Within minutes, he was sweating. His camouflage gear was soon damp. It was impossible to sprint. He jogged steadily, trying to regulate his breathing. Three paces as he inhaled. Three paces as he exhaled. His left ankle twinged from where he had hurt it on the snowy mountainside, but it seemed to be holding out. He tried to ignore the weight that could so easily drag him to the ground.

There were flags marking the way every two hundred metres. Max started to count them, but soon lost track. He was concentrating too hard on his breathing and his pace. They were all that mattered.

Ten minutes passed. Twenty. The shooting range slid past in his peripheral vision. The mountain slopes were a blur on either side. Max found himself in something like a trance. He kept a strict rhythm to his footsteps and his breathing. He tried to put all thoughts from his mind, apart from the thought of carrying on.

The terrain had been flat and sparse. Now he was heading slightly uphill. The extra exertion made his lungs burn. He was forced to slow down. His pace was little more than a fast walk. He felt a moment of panic. At this speed, he would never make it to the finish line in time. He forced himself to move faster. A minute later, he reached the brow of the incline and saw, a couple of hundred metres up ahead, the forest Hector had mentioned. The terrain ran downhill from there. That meant he could increase his speed. But not too much. Woody's advice still held. He had limited energy, which he had to conserve.

How far had he come? Five kilometres? Ten? He found it impossible to judge. Which meant he had no idea how much further there was to go. He hit the treeline of the forest and immediately realised he had a new obstacle. The ground was bumpy and knotty. He had to take care to keep his footing. He looked straight ahead. The forest was dense but the next flag was just visible, about fifty metres through the trees. Suddenly he felt overcome with exhaustion. *Just focus on the flag*, he told himself. If he could break the remainder of the exercise into small sections in his head, he had a much better chance of completing it in time.

Focus on the flag.

He gritted his teeth and kept his eyes level with the top of the flag. Distance: thirty metres.

Twenty.

Ten.

He reached it. Scanning ahead, he saw a flash of red: the next flag, half hidden in the trees.

Focus on the flag.

Breathing deeply, treading carefully, he ran towards it. He felt good. Breaking the forced march into little sections like this was doing the job. The flash of red grew closer . . .

Closer . . .

He was almost at the flag when it happened. Something caught his right foot. He stumbled and fell heavily. His face slammed hard against the ground. The weight of the full backpack winded him. But it was his left ankle that hurt the most. As he pushed himself up painfully, he realised he must have weakened it more than he thought.

He swore under his breath. How could he have been so stupid as to lose his footing? He looked down at the ground, trying to identify what had tripped him.

He saw it quickly enough.

He was standing between two trees. Running from one to the other, ten centimetres from the ground, was a length of rope. No, Max thought as he bent down to touch it. Not ordinary rope. Paracord.

He felt bile rising in his throat. Someone had tried to trip him.

Tried. And succeeded.

His eyes followed the length of the paracord from one tree to another. He saw a chewing-gum wrapper. It was lying on the ground near the cord. On closer inspection, Max saw that it was Lukas's brand.

Max felt hot with anger. Lukas had been weird with

him ever since he'd arrived. It was obvious that winning meant everything to him. To the extent that he was willing to do this . . .

For a moment, Max considered untying the paracord and taking it, along with the gum wrapper, as evidence that Lukas had sabotaged him. But he shook his head. That wasn't his style. He'd grown up learning to deal with his own problems. And since he was the last recruit, leaving it wouldn't compromise any of the others. So he turned his back on the clumsy booby trap and tried to continue running.

He winced. His left ankle was agony. He limped as he ran, and could only manage half his previous speed. He gritted his teeth and forced himself to carry on.

The going was slow and painful. The flags that marked his way seemed to take an age to reach and pass. He was sweating twice as badly now, and his breath came in short gasps. It took another twenty minutes to clear the forest. Only then did he see the finish line up ahead.

The others had all made it. They were standing in a little group slightly apart from Hector and Angel, next to the white minibus. Most of them were bent double, hands on knees, as they tried to get their breath back. Not Lukas. He was standing straight, looking back towards Max. As Max limped up to them, he saw that Lukas had a satisfied smile on his face.

'Good of you to join us,' Hector said. He clicked a

stopwatch and recorded Max's time in a notebook. Angel looked on sympathetically.

'What happened?' she asked.

Max glanced at Lukas. 'I tripped,' he muttered. 'It doesn't matter.'

'We'll get Martha to look at your ankle.'

'It doesn't matter,' Max repeated more forcefully.

'Everyone into the minibus,' Hector shouted. 'Move. Now.'

They bundled in. Max, limping, was last. He sat next to Abby and opposite Sami. As the minibus trundled back to the house, Sami looked at Max with an expression of sympathetic understanding. For the first time, Max felt irritated with his friend. He didn't need anybody's sympathy. He felt his face burning and he stared at the floor of the vehicle. Nobody spoke.

The journey back took fifteen silent minutes. Max's ankle throbbed. His anger failed to subside. He was still fuming as they disembarked at the parade ground and lined up at Hector's instruction. The Watcher looked at them all in turn. 'You've done well,' he said. 'Most of you, at least. Does anybody want to hand in their beret?' His eyes lingered briefly on Max. Max thought about doing it. Better to resign than to undergo the humiliation of being failed. But something stopped him. If there was just the smallest chance of success . . . Hector cleared his throat. 'All right. Those of you who've made it will be badged as Special Forces Cadets. Those of you who haven't will be going home.'

Max looked along the line. Lukas, Abby, Sami, Jack, Ash and him. Six recruits. They'd been told that only five would make it. One of them was about to receive bad news. Max had a pretty good idea who that would be.

'Lukas,' Hector said. 'You've impressed. Strength and endurance are good. Weapon handling skills are excellent. You think quickly and well. You're through.'

Lukas exhaled heavily. His shoulders seemed to relax.

'Sami. You fire a weapon better than I do, and that's saying something. You think on your feet, and you're stronger and fitter than you look. You're in.'

Sami smiled broadly. Then he looked sideways at Max and the smile fell away.

'Abby, good work. We'd have liked more girls. You were the only one who made the standard. You're joining us.'

Abby clenched her fist triumphantly and muttered something under her breath. Angel smiled at her.

'Jack, I'm not going to lie. For you it was touch and go. Your performance today dragged you over the line, but you're going to have to work hard. Welcome to the Special Forces Cadets.'

Jack had clearly only heard the good, not the bad. A self-satisfied expression spread over his face.

The four successful cadets had stepped back from the line. It was just Ash and Max left. Two recruits. One place left. Hector avoided their eyes as he consulted his notebook.

'Ash,' he said.

Max felt his stomach twist.

Hector continued to stare at his notebook for a moment, then he looked up. 'I'm sorry, mate,' he said. For the briefest moment, the older man looked regretful, even human. 'You were too slow today. Your weapons handling was so-so and you've been in the middle of the pack all along. We have to send you home.'

Ash hung his head. He looked genuinely crestfallen. Max felt for him. But he also felt a moment of elation. Because if Ash was out . . .

Hector turned to him. Max remembered what Hector had said on his first day here. *If you don't throw your hat in by the end of day four, I'll eat mine.* Well, Max hadn't thrown his hat in. He felt proud of that.

Hector looked him up and down. 'What happened today?' he said.

'I tripped,' Max said. He was on the verge of mentioning the paracord and the chewing-gum wrapper. But he kept that to himself. 'I think I twisted my ankle.'

'If you trip and twist your ankle on operations, you don't just compromise yourself, you compromise everyone on your team.' Hector's stare seemed to drill into Max.

'I understand,' Max said in a level voice. 'It won't happen again.'

'You're right there. It *won't* happen again. Your time was too slow today. You're not up to the level we require in the Special Forces Cadets. You need to forget all about what you've seen here. You're going home too.'

Max blinked at him. 'But . . . you said you needed five of us.'

'We need five cadets up to the correct standard. If we can't find them, we make do with fewer. There's no way we can keep you on the team. You'd just bring everyone else down with you.'

'But –'

'No buts. A helicopter will arrive at 10:30 tomorrow morning to take you and Ash back home. I'm sorry.'

Max stared dumbly at him. He couldn't think of anything to say.

'The rest of you, don't imagine this is the end. It's just the beginning. There will be a badging ceremony at 11:00 to officially confirm you as Special Forces Cadets. Then the work really begins. Continuation training starts as soon as these two have left. Get a good night's sleep. You're going to need it.'

Hector turned his back on them and marched towards the house. Woody and Angel exchanged a glance. They looked stunned. But they were evidently in no position to say anything. 'Come on, you lot,' Woody said quietly. 'Let's get you back to your huts.'

The others followed them across the parade ground.

Max stood, motionless, watching them go.

And as he watched, he wondered. What had he expected? That he was going to be lifted from his ordinary, friendless, family-free life and parachuted into something more exciting and meaningful?

Of course not. Stuff like that didn't happen to people like him. He felt stupid for even believing that might happen.

He was going home.

He had failed.

10

Green Thunder

It had been a long evening, and was turning into an even longer night.

Sami had been kind. As Max returned to the Nissen hut, his friend had come up to him and put one hand on his shoulder. 'Maybe they'll let you apply again,' he said.

'Yeah,' Max replied. 'Maybe.' He knew they wouldn't. He knew he'd blown it.

At dinner, the four successful recruits had sat together at the end of one long table. Max and Ash sat opposite each other, slightly apart from them. They weren't completely ignored. Sami kept trying to catch Max's eye. Abby made a pretence of not wanting her stew and offered it to Max. He declined. She wasn't fooling anyone.

He was still limping slightly as he left the dining room. 'You want me to strap that up?' Martha said, without much feeling, when she saw him.

'It's fine,' Max told her. She shrugged and walked away.

Back in the hut, Lukas refused, at first, to catch his eye. But that was impossible to maintain for long. Eventually, he surprised Max by offering his hand. 'No hard feelings, bro,' he muttered. Max looked at his hand but couldn't bring himself to shake it. Lukas shrugged and removed a piece of gum from his mouth. He wrapped it up and threw it on the floor. Then he went back to being his surly, uncommunicative self. Sami, who had been watching, looked like he wanted to intervene but thought better of it.

In the end, they all went to bed early. Max couldn't sleep. He was sure the same was true for the others, though nobody spoke. He simply lay there, staring into the darkness. His ankle throbbed, but that wasn't what kept him awake. He couldn't believe that he'd been given a chance to break out of his humdrum life and he'd messed it up. The three days of selection had been so busy that he hadn't realised how much he wanted this. Only now that it had been taken away was it clear to him what he had lost.

He'd lost everything.

He wanted to jump out of bed, storm across to the house and find Hector. Tell him about the paracord. Tell him that he'd been set up to fail. But he knew it would do no good. Hector had been against him since the beginning. He wasn't going to change his mind now. This was the result the grizzled Watcher had wanted all along. Max's failure was his success.

What would Max do now? That was the question that he kept coming back to. Sit it out at school until he could apply to join the army? Would they have him? he wondered. Would his failure here keep him out of the military for ever? He didn't know.

The night passed slowly. It was almost dawn when he started, finally, to nod off. He drifted in and out of sleep, reliving moments of the past few days. The abseil on Striding Edge. The battle through the snow. The gun work on the range. The heavy march through the forest. In his half-dreams he heard panicked shouting. The howling of the wind. The crack of firearms. And above it all, the constant thrum of a helicopter's rotor blades. Mechanical. Repetitive.

Nearby.

Max sat up, eyes wide. The hut had no windows, so it was dark inside, but he could see a faint grey outline around the door which told him it was morning. He could see the outlines of Lukas and Sami sitting up too. He frowned. Had the helicopter arrived already to take him and Ash back home? He checked his watch. It was eight thirty. Hector had definitely said ten thirty. Maybe the helicopter had just arrived early . . .

It sounded like it was hovering directly above them, and very low. The noise was thunderous. It seemed to make the whole hut shake.

'What's going on?' Sami shouted.

As if in reply, the door burst open. Light flooded in, and with it came Hector, followed by Woody and Angel. The older man's face was as thunderous as the noise above. 'Get out of bed!' he screamed. 'All of you! Get out of bed. Now!'

Sami almost fell out of bed. Lukas threw back the covers and stood up promptly, the muscles in his tattooed arm twitching.

Max didn't move. He felt rebellious. Why *should* he get out of bed? What authority did Hector have over him any more? Give it a couple of hours and Max would probably never see the guy again. He stayed put.

If anything, the din of the helicopter grew even louder. It seemed to be inside Max's head as well as outside. Hector strode up to him. 'What the hell do you think you're doing?' he yelled.

'Taking my time,' Max said.

Hector grabbed him by the arm and yanked him out of bed.

'Hey . . .' Max complained, but his complaint was drowned out by Hector screaming at him, his face close to Max's.

'Spare me your stupid teenage lip!' he bellowed. 'People are going to die!'

'Well, what's that got to do with me?' Max retorted.

'Did you hear what I said? People are going to die. Maybe they already have. Get dressed! Get out of here! Right now!'

'Mate, you've got to move,' Woody said. He was

standing at Hector's shoulder. 'Trust me on this. We'll explain in a minute.'

Max stared at him. He felt himself blush. Hector stormed back to the open door but Woody stayed where he was. His face, usually so open and friendly, was severe and urgent. It was that, more than anything, that made Max swing his legs over the side of the bed and start pulling on his camouflage gear. A minute later, he, Sami and Lukas were hurrying out of the Nissen hut. Abby was waiting for them. She was more dishevelled than usual and was nervously fiddling with the cartilage piercings in her left ear. Jack and Ash, bleary-eyed, were hurrying from another Nissen hut. Woody and Angel were carrying a large black flight case between them out of a third hut.

Hector was marshalling the helicopter on to the ground between the house and the huts. It was a Chinook, with the distinctive double rotors. Max wondered if it was the same aircraft that had brought him here from the Lake District. He certainly couldn't discern any difference. The downdraught from the rotors was strong. Sami shouted something at Max, but Max couldn't hear him. The noise was too great.

The Chinook touched down. Almost immediately, the tailgate lowered. Without hesitation, Woody and Angel ran their flight case up into the dark belly of the helicopter. Hector turned to the recruits and pointed after them. His lips mouthed the words, 'Get in!'

They looked at each other, nervous and confused. Lukas was the first to move. He sprinted up into the Chinook. Abby went next, then Sami and Jack. Max and Ash exchanged a long look. Max wondered if they were both thinking the same thing. What did this have to do with them? They were supposed to be going home . . .

Angel appeared at the top of the tailgate. She made an urgent 'get in' gesture to them. And then Hector was behind them, screaming. Max and Ash moved in unison, running up the tailgate and into the aircraft with Hector on their heel.

The others were sitting on low benches along the sides of the Chinook. There were two men in military gear that Max didn't recognise, both wearing chunky headsets. Max took a seat next to Woody as the tailgate started to close. He strapped himself in. There were headsets on the side of the chopper, each with a boom microphone. As the daylight diminished, Woody indicated to everyone that they should put them on. As Max did so, he felt the chopper leave the ground.

The headset was heavily cushioned so it softened some of the noise of the Chinook as it rose into the air. Max immediately heard voices.

– *This is Special Forces flight Green Thunder. We have our payload. Repeat, we have our payload.*

– *Receiving you, Green Thunder, you are cleared for flight.*

A pause, then the first voice came again.

– *Ladies and gentlemen, we have a flight time of approximately two hours. If we can shave anything off that, we will. Hector, you're patched into comms. It's all yours. Tell them what they need to know.*

11

Overruled

All eyes were on Hector. He sat at the end of the line opposite Max. Those sitting next to him – Lukas, Abby and Angel – had to crane their necks to see him.

'Can you all hear me?' Hector said. His voice was slightly scratchy over the headset, but it was clear enough despite the noise of the aircraft. Everyone nodded. 'Then listen carefully. We have a situation in London.'

'What sort of situation?' Abby said.

'This will be a hell of a lot more straightforward if you don't interrupt me.'

Abby looked chastened.

'At 08:00 this morning the Metropolitan Police received reports of a firearms incident at a London school.'

Hector let that sink in for a moment. Nobody interrupted.

'What I'm about to tell you is a mixture of eyewitness intelligence from the site, information gleaned from drone cameras, and analysis by MI5. The school in question is the Ashley Road Comprehensive. It is situated about a hundred metres from the Russian embassy.'

As he said this, he caught Sami's eye. Max glanced at his friend. Sami's expression was suddenly very hard. Hector moved on quickly. 'How many of you have heard of Chechnya?' He held up one hand. 'Don't answer that. I'm going to brief you about the situation anyway. The Chechen Republic is part of the Russian Federation. Chechen nationalists want their country to be separate from Russia. There is a long history of conflict between the two, but we're not here to take sides. Today is the final day of a Russian state visit to the UK. You may have read about it. There have been protests and some unrest by Chechens and those sympathetic to their cause. We believe that the situation at Ashley Road is linked to this'

'You mean, the gunmen are Chechen separatists?' Max said over the comms system.

'I thought we agreed I was going to talk and you were going to listen,' Hector replied.

Max flushed.

'But that is correct. What we have now is a siege situation. We think the Chechens have staged the siege to protest against the Russian state visit. The siege occurred a little before the school day started. Not all the pupils and teachers had arrived. There are approximately two hundred and fifty children between the ages of ten and sixteen, along with eight teachers, being held at gunpoint in the school. They include a group of Chinese exchange students. This makes the politics even more sensitive.'

Hector paused. He closed his eyes for a moment and took a deep breath, as though gathering his thoughts. He was obviously very tense.

'You may have heard of the Beslan school siege in 2004. It was a similar situation. Armed Chechen militants took over a school in the Russian town of Beslan. It lasted three days. There were more than a thousand hostages. In the end, Russian forces stormed the school. They were unprepared and heavy-handed. More than three hundred people were killed during the rescue, many of them children. It will be unacceptable for that to be repeated here in the UK.'

The recruits all stared at Hector in horror. He paused again before continuing.

'Professional hostage negotiators are on site, but the terrorists are currently refusing to engage with them. That means they don't want a compromise. They want the eyes of the world to be on them and to understand their protest against the Russians. It means things could turn very ugly. The SAS counter-terrorist team are on their way. They are the best-trained, best-prepared counter-terrorist team in the world. But they have one big problem.' He looked at each of the recruits in turn. 'They're adults.'

Hector let that sink in for a moment. There was a little turbulence. Nobody seemed to notice it. They were all staring at the Watcher.

'If the SAS go in blind,' Hector continued, 'we can't predict the outcome. We cannot risk the death of a hostage – and especially a child hostage – as a result of our rescue mission. We need eyes and ears on the ground. That is to say, inside the school. That's where you lot come in. We want to put you inside the school so you can relay information about the terrorists' numbers, actions and positions to our SAS counter-terrorist team.' He looked at them all in turn. 'It is very, very dangerous. This is a live situation. If the terrorists realise who you are and what you are doing, they will most likely start killing people. No prizes for guessing who will be top of their list.'

There was a silence. The Chinook shook with another burst of turbulence. Hector took a deep breath. He looked around the recruits again.

'You are untrained,' he said. 'Raw. You are wet behind the ears. Frankly, none of you knows what you are doing. It may be that by the time we land, the hostage negotiators will have done their job and the situation will be over. But the chances of that happening are vanishingly small. I'm going to be honest with you. If this was my call, I wouldn't be sending you in. The risk to you and to the operation is too great. But I've been overruled. You'll find that it happens quite a lot. None of you will ever meet the people I take my orders from. They like it that way, because it means they don't develop any personal feelings towards any of you. And *that* means they are more likely to send you into dangerous situations.'

Max found himself staring at Hector. The older man seemed to be revealing something new about himself. Until now, he had been harsh and unyielding. Suddenly, he had a glimpse of another side to Hector. A side that suggested he was more concerned about the recruits' well-being than he'd previously let on.

'Today is different,' Hector continued. 'It doesn't matter what my superiors say. It doesn't matter how much they try to overrule me. You are not yet officially Special Forces Cadets. You have not yet been badged. That means you are able to say no. If this operation sounds to any of you to be too dangerous – and I wouldn't blame you if it did – say the word and you will be pulled. No questions asked.' He sounded hopeful that they would do just that.

The recruits stared at him. For a good while, nobody spoke. Then, slowly, Max raised his hand.

Hector nodded curtly at him. If he had seemed to soften towards the others, he showed no sign of it with Max.

'I thought you said me and Ash weren't good enough,' Max said. 'What are we doing on this chopper? Why are we even involved?'

Hector looked from Max to Ash then back again. 'Right,' he said. 'If it was down to me, you'd still be on the ground. Seems I've been overruled for a second time. My superiors have decided, in their infinite wisdom, that numbers are important. The more eyes we have inside the school, the better. If you say yes, you're on the team. But for this job only. Don't get any ideas that this is a second chance. It isn't. Frankly, Max, it would be best if you said no right now. My superiors are making a mistake letting you near this operation. That's my honest opinion.'

Max felt himself flush. He looked round at Woody and Angel. They were avoiding his gaze, staring impassively into the middle distance. It was impossible to tell what they were thinking.

He became aware of Ash, his companion in failure, raising his hand.

'What is it, Ash?' Hector said.

'I'm not doing it,' Ash said quietly over the comms. At first he appeared nervous, but as the others looked at him his nerves turned to defiance. 'It's mad,' he said. 'You're all mad, if you do it. Armed terrorists? SAS teams? You reckon you can deal with that stuff just because you can run up a mountain?'

There was no reply. Ash bit his lower lip and clenched his fists.

'Seriously,' he persisted, 'it's crazy.' He waved an arm at Hector, Woody and Angel. 'They're all crazy.'

There was no response.

'What about you, Max?' Ash demanded. 'Surely *you're* not doing it? You heard what Hector said. What're you going to do, risk your life for nothing?'

Max narrowed his eyes. 'It's not for nothing, Ash,' he said. He looked at the other recruits. Lukas looked unconcerned but Max reckoned it was a mask. Beneath it, surely Lukas was nervous as hell, just like Max. Abby bit her lower lip, though her eyes were fierce. Sami, normally so open and friendly, had an unfamiliar hardness about him. Max felt he understood for the first time what the Watchers saw in him that made him so suited for this work. Jack looked eager. Cocky, almost. He hadn't endeared himself to Max so far, and he wasn't making things any better.

But none of them, he realised, shared Ash's opinion. They were quietly impressive as they sat in the belly of Green Thunder, clad in their camouflage gear.

They were also, Max realised, looking expectantly at him, waiting for his answer.

Max bowed his head. He realised he was scared. His limbs felt weak, his stomach twisted. He found himself thinking not of the school siege, nor of Valley House, nor even of the brutal selection process he had endured over the past three days. Instead, he thought of his room at the care home – the only place he really thought of as home. From here it felt safe. Warm. A million miles from talk of terrorists, sieges and automatic weapons.

It was also boring. Lonely. A dead end.

Max raised his head. He looked directly at Hector. Hector looked straight back.

'I'm in,' Max said.

He might have been imagining it, but as he spoke he saw something in Hector's expression. It was almost like desperation. But in an instant Hector had mastered it. He spoke into the comms again. 'We land in approximately ninety minutes,' he said. 'Ash will be escorted away from the team. The rest of you will receive further briefings on the ground. Prepare to move fast. The sooner you're on site, the sooner we can bring this thing to an end.'

12

Covert Comms

Green Thunder was losing height. Everyone in the chopper was on edge. Including the Watchers.

There was a judder as the Chinook's landing gear hit something solid. Max checked his watch: it was 11:15. The tailgate opened, letting in the bright morning light. For a moment, Max was confused. He could see rooftops and a vast cityscape. It was almost as though they were still flying. When Hector shouted at them to disembark, however, he realised they must have landed on the top of a tall building. Somehow that made him feel even more anxious.

Woody and Angel were already on their feet, carrying their flight case down the tailgate. Max and the others unclipped themselves. He, Jack, Abby, Lukas and Sami moved towards the tailgate. Ash hung back awkwardly. Max tried to move with purpose, hoping that it would give him more confidence. He was the first out of the chopper.

This rooftop landing zone was the highest point around. Max had never been to London before, but he identified the River Thames glittering in the sunlight. In the few seconds he had to look around, he saw landmarks he recognised from TV – the Houses of Parliament. St Paul's Cathedral. The Shard. Up here, there was no sense of movement down below, of anyone hurrying. He knew it was just a trick of the height. They were truly in the heart of the city.

The sky was clear but the wind was high. It wasn't simply the downdraught from the Chinook. The top of this building was buffeted from all sides. Max felt unsteady. He heard someone shout, 'Get off the landing zone!' Wind howled in his ears as he followed the instruction. He ran after Woody and Angel, who were carrying their flight case to the top of a stairwell at one edge of the building. The others followed. They descended several stone steps and went through a heavy metal door into the top floor of the building. Two military men were waiting for them at an open lift. Max, Woody, Angel and the other recruits crowded in. A minute later Hector joined them. There was no sign of Ash and nobody asked where he was. Max thought he could hear Green Thunder taking off, however. He figured Ash was still inside.

The lift took them to the ground floor in tense silence. The doors slid open on a large reception area that had evidently been cleared of any members of the public. There were glass windows on all sides, but they were blocked on the outside by six-foot-high screens. Beyond them, Max could see the blue neon flash of police lights. There was a distant sound of sirens.

Four people were waiting for them – three men and a woman. The woman took Abby and Angel to one side, out of sight. The men started to hand out casual clothes to the remaining boys.

'Get out of your camouflage gear,' one of them shouted. 'But don't start getting into these clothes yet.'

Max gave the others a sidelong glance. They were hesitating, clearly a little embarrassed about stripping. Max shrugged and removed his boots, jacket, T-shirt and trousers. By the time he stood in his socks and boxer shorts, the others had followed his lead. One of the three men approached him with a handful of wires and a roll of black duct tape. He handed Max a small box, no bigger or thicker than a fifty-pence piece. A black wire led from it. 'Tape this to the inside of your thigh, beneath your underwear,' the man said in a gruff, no-nonsense voice.

'What is it?' Max said.

'Communications wire and microphone. Highly advanced tech. Only available for high-level military operations. It'll allow us to hear what's going on in your vicinity.'

'Does it have to be placed there?' Max asked, pointing down at his boxers.

'Course not,' said the man. 'You can tape it to your nose if you want. But if you'd prefer to avoid being shot in the head, I'd put it somewhere out of sight in an area they're less likely to search.'

Max gave the sarcastic man a sour look. 'You a friend of Hector's?' he muttered, but didn't wait for a reply. He tore off a piece of duct tape and followed the man's instructions.

'We need to tape the wires up your chest,' the man said. Max threaded the wires through his boxers. The man tore off strips of duct tape and sealed the wires to his skin. He took another loop of wire and placed it over Max's head, round his neck, and connected it to the first wire. 'Induction loop,' he said. 'Okay, get dressed.'

The clothes he handed Max were exactly the right size. A pair of old jeans. A T-shirt and a threadbare V-neck jumper. Looking around, Max saw that the others had taped their wires to their bodies and were pulling on similarly nondescript clothes. Abby reappeared wearing jeans, a hoodie and a baseball cap. Max noticed that she'd removed her cartilage piercings. Made sense, he figured. They would have made her stand out. Her gait was slightly awkward. Max could tell she was wearing a wire too. He made a mental note to move as naturally as possible.

One of the guys approached holding something that resembled a matchbox. He opened it up. It was filled with cotton wool, and inside nestled a skin-coloured earbud. 'Put this in your ear,' he said.

'What is it?'

'Covert wireless earpiece. Invisible to the naked eye. Latest tech. Only available for . . .'

'. . . high-level military operations?'

'Right. You'll be able to hear your controller through it.'

'Can anybody hack into it?' Max had heard that this was possible.

'It's what we call secure covert comms,' the guy said. 'Encrypted at both ends. It's impossible to hack.'

Max took the earpiece and gingerly placed it into his ear. It was uncomfortable, and he felt sure that it must be very visible to anyone standing next to him. But the man looked and grunted in satisfaction before moving on to the others. The woman who had taken Abby away approached. She carried a pair of trainers. They were nothing fancy, and looked as if they had been well worn, with spots of mud here and there. She turned the left shoe upside down and twisted the heel clockwise. It clicked around to reveal a hidden compartment containing a razor blade and a small button compass. 'You try closing it,' she said, handing the shoe to Max. He took it and clicked the heel shut. 'Put them on,' the woman instructed. Max did as he was told.

The others were fitting their own shoes. Hector, Woody and Angel watched them. When they were done, Hector spoke. 'It's time to go. Follow me.'

They filed across the room to an exit guarded by an armed police officer. She gave the recruits a strange look as they walked past her, but said nothing. Waiting immediately outside was a white transit van, flanked by two police cars. The van's side door was open. The recruits and the Watchers entered and sat along either side of the van. Max noticed that they automatically took the same positions that they had on Green Thunder. Someone outside slid the door shut. Police sirens started up and the transit van moved away.

'We'll be on site in approximately fifteen minutes,' Hector announced. 'When we get there, you'll be shown a map of the school and be given a final briefing. In the meantime, I'm going to give you a crash course in communications. You're all wearing a wire. Once the operation starts, you'll be able to hear the control room and we'll be able to hear what you say and anything going on around you. Your microphones are very sensitive. They'll pick up what you say, even if you speak quietly. But you have to use your head. If the terrorists see you muttering to yourselves, they'll soon realise that something isn't right. That method of communication is only suitable if you're completely certain nobody is watching you.'

'What if somebody *is* watching us?' Abby said. She sounded stressed. Max was prepared for Hector to scold her for interrupting him, but he didn't.

'In that case, you speak out loud, but you do it in such

a way that nobody knows you're communicating with us. That means encoding your messages in some way.'

'What?' Jack scoffed. 'You want us to start talking gobbledegook over the microphone and hope *that* doesn't make people suspicious?'

Hector gave him a long look. The kind of look that could silence even a kid like Jack. Then he continued.

'The trick is to hide the message you want to transmit in normal-sounding conversation. For example, if you want to let us know that a child is hurt, say it to one of the terrorists. If they think you're having a conversation with them, they'll never guess that you're relaying information to us at the same time. Is that clear?'

They all nodded.

'In fact,' Angel added, 'talking to your captors is a good idea, if they let you. Hostage-takers don't want to think of their hostages as real people. If they do, it makes it harder to kill them when the time comes. Try to make friends. Talk about your family – real or invented. Talk about your hobbies and your life outside the siege. Don't allow them to dehumanise you. It won't work on all of them, but there's often a weak link somewhere in the terrorist team. You might be able to use that to your advantage.'

'Just be smart,' Woody said. 'Think carefully about whether you're softening the terrorists up or making them more aware of you – and therefore more likely to kill you when the shooting starts.'

'How do we know?' Sami asked.

'You don't,' Hector said grimly. 'You have to think on your feet.'

The police sirens stopped. Hector checked his watch. 'We should be there any moment,' he said.

A minute later, the van came to an abrupt halt. The side door slid open and an armed man in a black flak jacket, wearing a helmet with a boom mike, barked at them to follow him. The recruits bundled out. Max took in his surroundings. They were at the perimeter of the school. It was a network of ordinary-looking brick buildings surrounded by high green metal railings. They were alongside a playground with hopscotch and football pitch markings painted on the tarmac. Against a far wall was a huge, colourful painting that looked like it had been done by children. The area outside the railings was a mass of police cars and armoured military vehicles. There were perhaps thirty men and woman, all armed and flak-jacketed, talking into radios and calling instructions to each other. This area was cordoned off. There were no civilians. But Max could see, at the end of the road leading to the school, a guarded barrier. Here, members of the public were being held back. Max could see a couple of TV cameras. Instinctively, he turned away from them. He didn't want his face appearing on any news reports that the terrorists happened to be watching.

There was a newsagent's on the other side of the road. Hector led them into it. It had been turned into a makeshift operations centre, manned by about ten adults, some in police uniform, others in military gear. Cables snaked all over the floor, laptops had been set up in every available space, and a display board was propped up against the newspaper racks. It showed a set of building plans. They gathered round it.

'This is a plan of the school building,' Hector said. They all looked hard at it. The main buildings were shaped like a 'C'. Hector pointed out the furthest away line of buildings. 'This is the main teaching block,' he said. 'We believe it's deserted. We're calling it Block Red. The biggest room in the building is here.' He pointed to a large room on the south side of the school. 'This is the dining hall. It also doubles as a gym. There is a stage for plays at the east end, and it adjoins the kitchen at the west end. This is Block Green. Adjoining the north-west corner here is a toilet and shower block. Block Blue. To the best of our knowledge, the terrorists are holding the hostages in Block Green, the dining hall. Is everything clear so far?'

The recruits nodded.

'There are long windows along each side of Block Green,' Hector continued. 'These are covered with blinds. However, we have special optics available which allow us to see shadows through these blinds. At any one time, there appear to be three or four adults standing by them.

From the shape of their shadows, it looks like they're armed. So you need to infiltrate Block Green.'

'How are we supposed to do that?' Lukas asked. 'Walk up and knock on the door?'

The plans showed a main entrance to Block Green on the south side, from the playground. The railings that surrounded the school were marked on the plan. They formed a neat rectangle.

'We're here,' Hector said, pointing to the railings on the plan. 'The main entrance to the school is here, on the south-west corner. There's also a goods entrance here, behind this administrative building – Block Yellow. We've identified that as your best entrance. We have a nano drone up above it that tells us it's unmanned.' He pointed to one of the laptops, which showed clear aerial footage of a metal gate wide enough for a van to enter. The gate was closed and there was nobody in the vicinity.

'That doesn't make sense,' Max said.

Hector gave him a sharp look. 'Go on,' he said.

'Why is it so easy to get in? Why isn't there a gunman covering the entrance?'

'We don't know,' Hector said quietly. 'I guess we'll find out.' He cleared his throat. 'We'll get that gate open for you. You'll need to move behind Block Yellow then head straight into the teaching block. Follow the corridor that leads along the west side of the school and enter the toilet block by this entrance here.'

'How do we know the doors will be unlocked?' Abby asked.

'We've spoken to the school caretaker. He's confirmed that he unlocked the school fully this morning. We don't believe the terrorists have keys, but they may have barricaded themselves in.' He pointed at the map again. 'They will need to let the children out to use the toilet. That means there will be young people coming and going from Block Blue, the toilets, into Block Green, the dining room. You need to take advantage of that.'

'What if they're counting people in and out of the toilet block?' Max said.

'When you enter, we'll create a distraction in the opposite corner of the school. An explosion. That should get their attention and give you time to slip into the toilet block and from there into the main hall. Once you're inside, your objective is to give us full details of the situation. After that, you'll need to wait for further instructions. Are there any questions?'

There was an anxious silence.

Hector nodded. 'Good,' he said. 'We'll do a quick comms test. Then we're moving in.'

13

Advance to Target

The comms test took no more than five minutes. A voice Max didn't recognise spoke into his earpiece. The recruits replied. When they had confirmed that two-way communications were operational, Hector led them back to the transit van. Max heard someone wailing from behind the cordon. Maybe a family member of one of the hostages? Looking up, he saw two police helicopters circling. He realised he was sweating.

'We're taking the long way round to the north-west corner of the playground,' Hector explained as the transit moved away. 'The terrorists may have people beyond the cordon watching us. The driver will make sure we're not being followed, then will drop you a short walk from the goods entrance. You'll approach on foot.' He looked around at the recruits. 'It's not too late to drop out,' he said. 'If you're having second thoughts, say so now. This is the real deal.'

Silence.

It took five minutes to deliver the recruits to their

drop-off point. Max could feel the vehicle circle a roundabout several times to flush out anyone following them. When they came to a halt, Max checked the time. 12:57. A voice came over his earpiece.

– *This is Zero Alpha. Do you copy, Cadet Force?*

The recruits looked at each other uncertainly.

'Roger that,' Max replied tentatively. He found that the military jargon came naturally to him.

– *Drone footage shows that the access route is clear. Advance to target. Repeat, advance to target.*

'Go!' Hector barked as the transit door slid open. And as they bundled out of the van, he shouted again. 'Hey!'

The recruits turned to look at him.

'Stay alive, recruits. Remember, this is not an exercise.'

He looked grim. It wasn't the most encouraging send-off Max had ever heard.

Woody and Angel were waiting outside the van. They were in a deserted, litter-strewn street with three-storey townhouses on either side. Angel pointed. 'That way,' she said quietly. 'The area has been cleared. We're inside the police cordon so you shouldn't see any members of the public. Take a left at the end. You'll see the goods entrance. Go carefully and stay in contact as much as you can.' She fist-bumped each of them in turn. 'And guys: work together, okay? That's the most important thing. You're a team now.'

The truth was, they didn't feel like a team to Max. He

sensed that both Lukas and Jack saw themselves as leaders. They almost shoulder-barged each other as they ran in the direction Angel had indicated. Max, Sami and Abby followed. At the street corner they all stopped and looked to the left. Sure enough, there was the goods entrance to the school. There was a large area of tarmac beyond it, leading to the administration offices: Block Yellow.

It was strangely quiet. Apart from the distant hum of the circling helicopters, Max could hear nothing. He would have expected a terrorist incident to be noisier. But it was the silence, he realised, that was so strange. This was the middle of London. It was supposed to be noisy and busy. It was dead quiet because something was very wrong.

'We should go one by one,' Max said. 'That way, if one of us is spotted . . .'

'Yeah, I get it,' Lukas said without looking at him. 'I'll go first.' It was weird, hearing his voice both in real life and over the comms earpiece.

Without waiting for a reply, Lukas ran in the direction of Block Yellow. Despite his muscular build, he was fast and light of foot. As soon as he reached the building, he hid on the side furthest from the main school block. It meant he was out of sight of the other recruits, but they heard his voice over the comms.

– *It's me, Lukas. I'm in position on the west side of Block Yellow.*

– *Roger that.* The comms reply was crackly.

Abby went next, then Sami. Max and Jack watched them go. When they were alone, Jack turned to Max. 'Do what I tell you in there,' he said, very quietly so that the comms team would have trouble hearing him. 'Remember that you didn't pass selection. You're not really one of us.'

Max tapped his earpiece, as if to say, 'I'll do what the Watchers tell me.' They heard Sami's voice.

– *In position.*

Jack scowled at Max, then ran towards Block Yellow.

It felt weird, being on his own. The silence was oppressive. Max looked back over his shoulder. That way lay safety. In the school, danger. He could still choose one over the other, if he wanted . . .

Jack's voice over the comms.

– *In position.*

Which meant it was Max's turn to go. He sprinted through the school gates, scanning the area ahead as he ran, looking for any movement or threats. There were none. He found the others with their backs to the wall on the west side of Block Yellow.

'Don't you think it's weird,' Max said quietly, 'that we can enter the school grounds so easily? You'd think the terrorists would have guards or lookouts or something.'

'They're probably scared of snipers,' Sami said.

'Yeah, maybe,' Max said. 'But I think it means they're very sure they've got all the kids under control, and that they can do something pretty bad if they suspect a rescue team is coming in.'

Nobody had an answer to that. Lukas and Jack didn't even seem to have heard what Max said. Lukas took the lead again. He led them round the north end of the building and pointed at a door to the main teaching block. 'I'm going to check it's unlocked,' Lukas said. 'If it is, follow me in.'

Max was about to say, 'If we don't start working together, this is going to end badly . . .' But he didn't get the chance. Lukas didn't wait for anyone to agree or disagree with the plan. He simply sprinted across the open ground to the door. He opened it and slipped inside. Without waiting for any kind of agreement, the others followed, in the same order as before. Again, Max found himself momentarily alone, scanning the area carefully. Nothing. Just that uncanny silence. If he didn't know what was really happening, he'd think the school was deserted.

When Jack had disappeared into the building, Max followed. He felt vulnerable running across the open tarmac. Instinctively, he ran crouched over, to present a smaller target, just in case. But he reached the building unharmed.

He found himself with the others in an empty corridor with a shiny grey vinyl floor. The lights were on. The walls were covered with children's artwork: collages and pastel drawings. There were classrooms on either side of the corridor. By each classroom was an alcove where the children had messily stashed their bags and coats. There was a familiar smell. It was a mixture of poster paints and cleaning products that Max recognised from his own school.

Once again, Lukas took the lead. They followed him along the corridor. Max had a good sense of direction. He knew they were heading south, and his memory of the school plan was clear. As they passed the classrooms and alcoves, he realised that the kitchen was up ahead and the toilet block was at the end of the corridor on their left. Their feet echoed as they hurried in that direction. Anxiety rose in Max's gut like bile. It went against every instinct to head towards danger rather than away from it. But right now, that was their job.

They reached the door to the toilet block. It had stick drawings of both a boy and a girl on it. Lukas pushed it very slightly to check it was unlocked.

The door remained firmly shut. It was locked.

The recruits stared dumbly at it. What now?

Jack pointed to the end of the corridor. There was a door marked 'Kitchen: Staff Only'. They knew from the school plans that the kitchen led directly into the dining hall where the hostages were being held. Lukas and Jack looked at each other, as if silently conferring without any input from the others.

'I don't think we should go in via the kitchen,' Abby said. 'There could be guards in there.'

Hector's voice came over the comms.

– *Cadet Force, what's your status?*

'The toilet block is locked,' Jack said.

– *Wait.*

There was a short pause. The cadets stood silently, unsure what to do. Then Hector's voice came over the comms again.

– *The caretaker must have forgotten to unlock the toilet door. You're going to have to access Block Green through the kitchen. Enter the kitchen one by one. When you're all in there, we'll create a distraction in the south-east corner of the school. Move, now.*

The recruits looked at Lukas. He didn't seem so keen to be the first one in any more. 'I'll do it,' Max offered. But that seemed to change Lukas's mind. He shook his head and led them all to the kitchen entrance. Cautiously he opened the door and peered inside. Max couldn't see through the gap in the door, but he caught a faint whiff of yesterday's lunch. He felt a bizarre pang of hunger as he realised he hadn't eaten since the previous night.

Lukas entered the kitchen. The other recruits heard him say, 'It's clear.' Then, one by one, they slipped in after him: Abby, Sami, Jack. Max was preparing to head in after them when his heart almost stopped.

– *What are you doing in here? Who are you?*

The voice in Max's earpiece was harsh and foreign. Max shrank back from the kitchen door. He looked around.

His eyes fell on the alcove next to the nearest classroom. It was a mess of bags and coats. He ran towards it, squeezed himself into the corner and covered himself with coats. As he hid, he could hear events unfolding in the kitchen over his comms.

– *I said, what are you doing in here?*

It was Abby who spoke next. She sounded terrified.

– *We were trying to escape. We sneaked into the kitchen when you weren't looking.*

It was a good call, Max thought. Make the terrorists think that they were trying to break out, not break in. With so many children inside the hall, they surely wouldn't be able to recognise them all.

– *How many others?*

– *None.*

That was Sami's voice.

It's just us.

– *Stupid children.*

Max heard the door open. He held his breath and kept very still. His skin prickled. He could tell the owner of the voice was looking out into the corridor.

Ten seconds passed.

Twenty.

He heard the door close and exhaled very slowly. Then he heard the foreign voice again.

– *Get back in there with the others, or I'll shoot you here!*

130

There was a scuffling sound over the comms. Max pictured his four companions being bundled into the dining room. Even now he didn't move. His brain was all over the place. What should he do? Run away? Go after them? Could he really risk trying to enter from the kitchen now?

He spoke quietly. 'It's Max. The others have been captured.'

Hector's voice was tense.

– *Where are you?*

'Hiding in the corridor.'

– *Stay there for now. The rest of you, listen up. I know you can't reply at the moment, but I want you all to keep an eye on the door to the kitchen. If any of you see that it's not being watched, cough three times. Max, when you hear that signal, move into the kitchen. When you're in position, let us know. Wait until you hear another three coughs, then enter Block Green. Is that understood?*

'Weren't you going to create a distraction?'

– *This is better, now we have people on the inside.*

'If you say so.' It hardly sounded foolproof to Max.

– *Then stand by. And Max?*

'Yeah?'

– *This is not a time for errors.*

Thanks for the warning, Max thought, but he didn't say it.

Time passed. Max didn't know how long. Five minutes?

Ten? Over the comms, he could hear a low hum of voices from inside the dining room. The occasional person shouting for quiet. A low hum of other voices. Crying. When the three coughs came, however, they were louder than the other noises. Max couldn't identify who had given the signal. Sami, perhaps. He emerged from his hiding place and, checking he was still alone, crept to the kitchen door. He took a deep breath, then stepped inside.

The kitchen was immaculate. There were metal counters and huge pots and pans on shelves, but no sign of food preparation. Max guessed the terrorists had struck before the kitchen staff had started to prepare lunch. There was a metal partition between the kitchen and the dining hall, but it was shut. A single door in one corner was the only way in. Max approached it.

'I'm by the door,' he said into the comms. 'Give me the all-clear when nobody's looking towards it and I can enter without being seen.'

There was a moment of silence. Then three more coughs.

'Here goes nothing,' Max muttered to himself. He opened the door and slipped into the dining room.

14

Block Green

The first thing Max noticed was the fear. You couldn't see it. You couldn't hear it. But you could certainly sense it. The air was thick with terror, like a cloud of invisible gas.

Before even scanning the room, Max put his back to the wall next to the door and slid down to the floor. There were several other kids sitting cross-legged near the door. A couple of them noticed him. He made a shushing gesture at them. They lowered their heads. They looked as if they didn't want to draw attention to themselves. He looked around to check that none of the adults in the room had noticed his entrance. He was sure they hadn't.

Hector's intel had been good. There were indeed about two hundred and fifty children in the dining hall. They were sitting in groups – not classes, because the kids in each group were all of different ages, and the groups were of different sizes. Many of the younger kids were crying. Some of the older kids were doing what they could to comfort them. Arms round shoulders. Quiet words of encouragement. But the older kids were plainly terrified too, and the younger ones could tell.

Along the left-hand wall was a door with a toilet sign over it. Max knew that led to the area they hadn't been able to access. Three tearful young kids – two boys and a girl – were standing in a line outside it. They were the only children standing up. Everyone else was cross-legged or on their knees. A few of the younger ones were lying down.

Max looked around for the terrorists. They weren't hard to spot. There were fifteen in total. They wore blue overalls, like car mechanics, and black balaclavas. The only visible parts of their faces were their eyes and mouth. Some of them carried submachine guns. Max recognised the guns as MP5s, the same weapons they'd used on the range back at Valley House. Others had pistols, which he couldn't identify.

Eight of the gunmen had their weapons taped to their hands with thick black duct tape. He didn't understand why. These gunmen were standing, spaced out, along the two long walls of the hall. Actually, Max thought, perhaps they weren't all gun*men*. Four of the figures looked, from their shape, female. But it was hard to be sure with their heads covered.

Max looked for the other recruits. At the far end of the dining hall there was a raised stage, about a metre and a half high. It had thick red curtains on either side and a painted backdrop for a school play. Lukas, Sami, Abby and Jack were on the stage. They were kneeling with their hands behind their heads. Lukas looked angry, Sami strangely passive, Abby defiant and Jack very scared. None of them was able to speak over the comms; a terrorist was walking up and down the stage in front of them, keeping an eye on them. He carried an MP5.

Automatically, Max started assigning labels to each of the terrorists. He called the figure standing on the stage, keeping watch over Lukas, Abby and Sami, T1. He continued clockwise around the room until he reached T15. In truth, there was little to distinguish them. The figures he thought were female were T5, T8, T9 and T10. T7 looked male but was slightly smaller than the others.

Max turned his attention to the rest of his surroundings. Each of the long walls had a window that ran almost the entire length of the hall. Neither of these windows let in any light. As Hector had informed Max and the others, the windows were covered with fitted blinds that blocked out all daylight. The room was illuminated by strip lighting along the ceiling. Max assumed that the blinds were there so the hall could be darkened for school plays. Today they served the purpose of ensuring that nobody could look in, or out, of the dining hall. Max noticed, however, that the figures with the weapons taped to their hands stood in front of the blinds. Again, he wondered why.

The toilet door opened. Another gunman appeared: T16. He let a couple of kids back out into the hall before roughly pushing the two boys in the queue into the toilet block and following them in.

There was so much here that scared Max: the sinister balaclavas, the evil-looking firearms, his companions' desperate situation. But there was something else that chilled him more.

Eight of the terrorists – T1, T3, T6, T7, T11, T12, T14 and T16 – were wearing black padded vests. They were obviously stuffed with explosives: Max saw an orange-coloured plastic substance emerging from some of the pouches, and the vests themselves were a tangle of wires.

He knew what they were: suicide vests.

His eyes moved from the vests to the dining hall at large. He saw more wires. They were tied from wall to wall. Where they criss-crossed the hall they were above everybody's heads. Where they snaked around the perimeter they were loose on the floor. At intervals along the two side walls the wires fed into rough packages on the ground. Each of these packages was about the size of a football. They comprised more of the orange plastic explosive, wrapped up in duct tape. Each package had a narrow cylinder of metal inserted into the explosive and connected to the wires. Max knew that these were detonators. The packages were improvised explosive devices. Bombs. The entire dining room was rigged to blow up. He counted six devices in all. If they went off, it would be a bloodbath.

He blinked at the devices, then looked back at the suicide vests. A horrifying thought occurred to him. What if the terrorists only intended for this to siege to finish one way? What if they had no intention of leaving anybody in the school alive, and every intention of taking the hostages with them when they went? What if they *wanted* a rescue team to rush in, so they could explode the devices, kill more people and gain more attention for their cause? That could explain why it had been so easy to enter the school grounds.

He had to warn Hector.

The nearest gunman, T6, was about fifteen metres away. Max reckoned that, if he bowed his head, he could speak quietly without being noticed. 'It's Max,' he murmured. 'I'm in –'

Before he could say more, he was interrupted. The gunman on the stage – T1 – spoke out loudly. He had a strong accent – Chechen, Max supposed – but his English was good. Max could hear him clearly. 'Maybe some more of you would like to try to escape, like these idiots,' he announced.

A breathless hush descended on the hall. There was still the sound of crying from the younger ones, but it was clear everyone was listening.

'I will show you what happens when you try to do that,' the gunman said.

– *What's going on?* Hector's voice was urgent over the comms, but Max couldn't reply. T6 had walked towards him and was well within earshot.

T1 looked along the line of recruits on their knees, pointing at each of them with his MP5, as if choosing one. They all looked straight ahead, not wanting to catch his eye. The barrel of the MP5 finally rested on Jack.

'You,' the gunman said. 'Stand up.'

Jack stood. His knees were visibly trembling. He looked as if he might collapse with fear.

The gunman turned to face the dining hall. 'Choose one,' he instructed.

'What do you mean?' Jack replied.

'Are you stupid? Choose one of these children. Then I will kill them, as a punishment for your attempt to escape.'

Jack looked at him in horror. Then he shook his head. 'No,' he said.

'You are refusing to do as I say?'

'They haven't done anything wrong. I'm the one who tried to escape. Not any of them.'

It was absolutely silent in the room now. There was not even any crying.

Max could see the gunman's lips curl into a sneer. 'Ah!' he said. 'A hero! Very well.' He put the barrel of the MP5 to the side of Jack's head. 'I shall punish you instead.'

Max wanted to shout out, but he was paralysed with shock and fear. The other recruits looked on in terror. Jack closed his eyes.

It all happened very quickly. The gunman spun round his MP5 and held it in both hands. He whacked the butt of the weapon against the side of Jack's head. There was a sickening crack. Jack went down immediately, toppling from the stage onto the floor, landing hard. There was a collective moan from the hostages in the room. Lukas, Sami and Abby craned their necks over the edge of the stage, looking horrified. Max could see nothing above the heads of the other hostages. Half of him wanted to get to his feet so he could see Jack. Half of him wanted to vomit. He did neither, but stayed crouched on the ground, head bowed, limbs weak.

'He was lucky,' the gunman on the stage announced. 'If anyone else tries to escape, I will use the other end of the weapon.'

More panic in the room. Max looked up. The other recruits were still on their knees, their hands behind their backs. They were all staring at Max. Max put his hand over his mouth. 'Stop staring at me,' he hissed into the comms. The other recruits immediately looked down.

He couldn't say any more. T6 had turned his way again

and was walking towards him. Instead, Max slid across the floor to one of the other students, a ginger-haired boy about his own age. Taking advantage of the increased noise in the room, he struck up conversation. 'These wires going overhead and all around the room, do you know what I think they are?'

The boy gave him a strange look. 'Who are you? I don't recognise you,' he said.

'I'm new today,' Max said. He gave a little grimace. 'Great day to start a new school, huh?'

'What are they?' the boy asked.

'Look, they lead to those packages all around the room. I think they're bombs. I think the whole place is rigged to blow up.'

– *How many devices, Max?*

'I've counted them,' Max said to the boy. 'There's six. That must be enough to take the roof off this place.'

Max thought the ginger-haired boy couldn't have turned any paler. He was wrong. The boy looked down at the floor, as if he couldn't bear to look at Max or at the wires. Max didn't like worrying the kid, but he had to get the intel to the Watchers somehow.

'Why do eight out of the sixteen terrorists have their guns taped to their hands anyway?' Max continued. The more information he could relay to Hector, he figured, the better. 'I wish they'd all take their balaclavas off so we could see their faces . . .'

'Quiet!' T1 shouted. For a short while, it had the desired effect. He couldn't stop the little kids crying, however, and after a few seconds the low-level hum of voices started up again. The ginger-haired boy put his hand up. T6 approached. Max held his breath. What was the kid doing? Did he suspect Max? Was he going to tell the terrorists that Max had been quizzing him? His heart thundered in sudden panic as the gunman stood over them.

'I need the toilet,' the boy said quietly. The gunman pulled him unsympathetically to his feet and pushed him in the direction of Block Blue, where he queued with a couple of others.

In the middle of the dining hall was a group of about ten students. One of them stood up. She looked Chinese, as did everyone in her group. Max remembered Hector saying that there were some Chinese exchange students at the school. This girl had long dark hair, very straight, and her features were hard and cold. She crossed over to a group of younger children and said something waspishly to them. The terrified kids fell silent. Then the Chinese girl picked her way through the hostages towards the stage. There were steps on the right-hand side. Head high, the girl mounted them. All eyes were on her as she approached T1. She spoke to him. There was no way Max could tell what she was saying. For a moment, he wondered if she was brave or stupid. But as T1 nodded and a smug smile spread across the girl's face, it became clear to Max what she was doing.

T6 had moved away. None of the other terrorists was in the vicinity, so he was able to speak, but he had to be subtle. He put his head in his hands, as if in desperation. He didn't have to act too hard.

'One of them hit Jack in the head with the butt of his gun.' He heard the edge of panic in his voice. 'I don't know what state he's in. He's definitely unconscious. He . . . he might even be dead – he fell heavily off the stage. A Chinese girl is on the stage now. She's talking to the main guy. I think she's trying to collaborate with the terrorists. You know, offer to help them in return for saving her own skin. I mean, it's stupid, because obviously they won't let her go. She's going to end up dead like the rest of us.' The panic in his voice had increased.

Silence.

'Hector?'

The Chinese girl was stepping down from the stage. She started to walk around the dining hall with an air of authority. Wherever she went, children fell silent and looked at the ground. But one child, crouching very close to where Jack had fallen, cried out, 'His nose is bleeding! Look! He's not breathing! I think he's dead!'

T1 shouted at the kid to be quiet. Max barely heard. The room was spinning. Again he wanted to vomit. Could

Jack really be dead? Was that the fate that awaited them all? He was weak with fear.

'Hector! What do we do?'

No reply.

'Woody? Angel? Can anyone hear me?'

A wave of desperation overcame him. There was nothing he *could* do. There was nothing *any* of them could do.

'This is hopeless,' he whispered into the comms. He felt a moment of sudden anger. 'What were any of you even thinking?' he hissed at the silent Watcher. 'Sending a bunch of kids into a situation like this to save the day? We're going to die just like all the others. The whole place is booby-trapped. There are sixteen armed terrorists. Eight of them are wearing suicide vests. It's obvious what they're doing, isn't it? They're just *waiting* for an assault. And we're not superheroes or something. We're just a bunch of kids.' He drew a deep, shaky breath. 'Special Forces Cadets?' he spat dismissively. 'We're just a bunch of kids who are going to die, and it's all your fault.'

There was silence over the comms.

'Hector? Are you even there?' He looked up. The other recruits on the stage were a picture of terror. Even Lukas's eyes were wild. None of them could take their eyes off Jack. Max had the impression they were all feeling the same way as him.

– *Have you quite finished?*

Hector's voice was very calm. Max didn't reply. He couldn't, because T6 was approaching again.

– *Good. Then my advice is to shut up and listen. I've got something to tell you all.*

15

The Past

For the next few minutes, Hector spoke in a quiet, calm voice over the comms system. Max wasn't fooled, however. He could tell that beneath his gruffness there was a quiver of emotion. Maybe it was fear. Maybe it was something else.

– I'm not going to pretend that this is going the way we hoped. This situation is even graver than we thought and our options are limited. They depend on you and your ability to trust each other and yourselves. I've met a lot of military personnel. The best operatives have this in common: absolute trust in their own ability and absolute trust in their team. You haven't had time to build that trust, so I'm going to tell you now why I know you're up to this task.

When you all arrived at Valley House, we told you the rules. You weren't to talk about your backgrounds or family history to anyone. There were good reasons for that. Now there are good reasons for you to learn about each other.

Let's start with Lukas. Maybe some of you noticed his tattoos. Certainly you can all tell he has an American accent. You might even have heard of the place he comes from. Compton, Los Angeles.

Max looked across the room at Lukas. His face was hard and emotionless. Max had the impression that, whatever Hector was about to say, Lukas didn't want it to be heard.

– Compton is gang territory. Walk round the corner into a street governed by a different gang, you're dead. End of story. There's more gun crime in those streets than almost anywhere else in the world. If any of you were wondering why Lukas was so good with a weapon, now you know. In his world, handguns are as common as toothbrushes: everybody has one. Those tattoos on his arms are gang tattoos. He's had them since he was nine. His mum and dad had them too. That's why they were killed.

Lukas's eyes tightened. His jaw clenched.

– Their killer was a rival gang member. A scumbag with more than ten killings to his name. Everybody knew it was him, including the Los Angeles Police Department. But the killer was well hidden in the heart of his gang community, and the police weren't going to risk their own skins for yet another gangland shooting. If the killer was going to be brought to justice, someone else would have to do it.

That's what Lukas did. In the dead of night, he entered the rival gang's territory. He broke into the apartment where his parents' killer lived. Then he forced him, at gunpoint, to leave. A lesser guy would have taken the killer back to his own gang's territory and let his people deal with them. Lukas took him downtown to the LAPD. The killer is now serving life.

Lukas's expression hadn't changed. Abby, next to him on the stage, glanced at him in amazement. Max tried not to show any emotion because T6 was watching him. It was hard. He was having to change how he thought about Lukas in almost every respect.

– Trouble was, Lukas knew his own gang wouldn't take kindly to him having contact with the police. So he couldn't go back home. But by that point he was on the radar of the British security services. We spread our net wide. Lukas was orphaned. Smart. Skilled. Just the type we were looking for. I knew from the moment he arrived at Valley House that he'd make it through selection. The rest of you, you want to understand why Lukas was so keen to succeed? Now you know. The alternative was going back to Compton. And that was no alternative at all. Lukas, I know you can't talk at the moment and I don't know what you're thinking. But I do know this: you're a match for these terrorists.

Hector paused. Max felt his pulse rate increase. The Chinese girl was looking directly at him from across the room, suspicion in her eyes. Max looked away as Hector continued.

– Abby. You've been a fighter for as long as you can remember, right? You've had to be. Can't have been easy, being born in prison. Especially a tough, sectarian prison in Northern Ireland. Abby's mum was doing time for murder. She was pregnant with Abby when the sentence started and Abby was a prison child for the first few years of her life. After that, she went to live with her grandmother. Not easy, is it, Abby, fighting off the other kids, who victimise you because your mum's a murderer? You've got a police record as long as your arm. Hardly surprising, when you have to fight just to be able to walk to school. Most employers would take a dim view of a record like that. Not us. We had our sights on you even before your grandmother died, Abby. You're clever and fierce and independent. Like Lukas, it was obvious you'd make it through selection the moment you arrived at Valley House. You had the swagger. And I know something else. The people taking over this school are just bullies. Sure, they're bullies with guns and explosives, but they're bullies all the same. You've already shown that you can deal with people like that.

Abby was staring into the middle distance. Max had no way of telling what effect Hector's words were having on her.

– I bet a few of you thought Sami was never going to make it through selection, right? Too small, too lightweight, too damn nice. Well, let me tell you this: Sami's one of the toughest guys I've ever met, and I've

met a few. He comes from Syria. His father was a leading anti-government protester. In Syria, that's a dangerous thing to be. When things went bad in his country, Sami's family were forced into hiding in the town of Aleppo. Maybe some of you have heard of it. If you look at pictures of Aleppo now, you won't find a single building still standing. That was Sami's home for two years.

Sami, as always, was unable to hide his emotions. If anybody else in the hall was looking at him, they'd think he was scared. Max realised it was something else.

– *Sami's father managed to stay alive for six months. But the building in which they were hiding was hit by a government air strike. One bomb killed a hundred and thirty-eight people, including Sami's dad. His mother and two sisters survived, but they were all still on the government's hit list. Sami moved them to a new hiding place and protected them from government troops for nine months. You want to know why he was even better than Lukas on the range? It's because he spent those nine months with an AK-47 in his hand, protecting his family from people who wanted to kill them. I don't know how many government troops he was forced to shoot. I'll never ask him, and I hope none of you do either, when you get out of here.*

Tears ran down Sami's cheeks. The Chinese girl, who was striding up and down in front of the stage and did not know the real reason Sami was upset, sneered at him.

– It was another air strike that killed what was left of Sami's family. After that there was nothing to keep him in Aleppo. He made the dangerous journey from Syria across Europe to the UK. We picked him up when he claimed asylum. I guess I don't need to explain why he's exactly the type of person who would thrive in the Special Forces Cadets.

There was a moment of silence. In one corner of the hall, four terrorists were conferring. A couple of them looked at their watches. Max wondered why. He felt a wave of sickness. Were they on a schedule?

He was distracted by Hector's voice again.

– Jack's out of the game. We don't know if he's alive or not. There will be time later to mourn him if he isn't. Which leaves Max.

Yeah, Max thought. Which leaves me. No grand backstory. No tales of incredible courage. I'm an orphan, sure, but there's nothing special about me. No wonder I didn't pass selection, if that was what the Watchers were looking for.

– Maybe I should have told you this before, Max. I knew your dad.

Max suddenly felt disconnected from everything that was happening around him. He couldn't hear the crying of the kids. He barely saw the terrorists, or even felt the danger he was in. He was aware of nothing but Hector's voice. 'What?' he whispered, not even bothering to hide the movement of his lips. T6 looked at him sharply, but then lost interest.

– *He was a soldier, Max. A damn good one. Probably the best I ever met. I served with him in Afghanistan. Before that in Iraq. He was always the first man in and the last man out. Brave to a fault. Like his son, from what I've seen. And you know what I'm wondering now? I'm wondering, what would he think if he knew that his boy was doubting himself? What would he think if he knew that you were considering giving up now, when so many people's lives are at risk, and they all depend on you? Because, make no mistake, if you four fail, this siege will end only one way: in innocent people being killed. You may be killed. It's you, or it's them.*

Max was stunned into stillness. He had a thousand questions, but he couldn't ask a single one. In his mind's eye he saw a soldier, tired and dirty, in the battlegrounds of Afghanistan. The soldier was older than him, but looked like him. He was, Max realised, the person whose photograph he had seen on the wall in Valley House. In Max's imagination, the soldier looked back at him with a calm, confident expression. An expression that said, *you can do this* . . .

Max's attention cut back to the real world. The Chinese girl was shouting at a young boy to be quiet. The kid had lost it and was shouting out in panic.

'I want to go home! *Let me go home!*'

T3 and T11 strode up to him. One pulled the kid up by his collar. The other cuffed him round the side of the head. A few children started crying again. The Chinese girl looked on with her familiar smug expression.

Something snapped inside Max. He looked across the hall at the others. They looked back. Hector's pep talk appeared to have done the trick. Lukas, Abby and Sami were looking at the Chinese girl with undisguised contempt. Their demeanour had changed. They were no longer cowed. They were steely and confident. Max locked gazes with each one in turn. Almost imperceptibly, Sami, Abby and Lukas nodded back at him.

Max buried his head in his hands once more, as if in distress. He put all thoughts of his father from his mind. There would be time enough to think about that when they got out of here.

Which they would.

Unobserved by T6, he spoke quietly over the comms. 'What do you need us to do?' he said.

16

T7

Hector continued to speak in a calm, insistent voice.

– *First things first. The terrorists with guns taped to their hands. They're not terrorists at all. They're probably teachers. They've been dressed up in balaclavas and overalls and had the weapons fixed to them to make us* think *they're terrorists. They're decoys. It's a common trick. The terrorists know that we might have snipers trained on them. By dressing up some of their hostages, they increase the chance that we shoot the teachers instead of them.*

'Nice,' Max breathed.

– *The Chinese girl you mentioned? It's possible she's displaying signs of Stockholm Syndrome. That's when hostages start sympathising with, and even admiring, their captors. Be extremely wary of that girl, but watch out for the signs of Stockholm Syndrome in yourselves. It's a very real thing. If you start feeling sympathy for any of these terrorists, remember: these people woke up this morning intending to kill children.*

From now on, I will refer to the teachers as decoys and the real terrorists as targets. But our first priority is going to be neither the decoys nor the targets. It's going to be the IEDs – the improvised explosive devices. Max, we agree with your analysis. We think the targets are waiting for our assault team to make a move. As soon as there is any sign of that, they're going to detonate the IEDs and their suicide vests. It's a way of increasing the collateral damage and gaining more publicity for their cause. It makes it look like the atrocity is our fault. We're working on a strategy for taking out the targets individually, but first we need to disable the IEDs – because if they explode, nothing else matters. Max, the next voice you hear will be Angel's. She's a demolitions expert. She'll talk you through it.

Max didn't say anything. For the second time, the Chinese girl was looking straight across the hall at him. He couldn't let her see him move his mouth. He let Angel do the talking.

– Max, we think all the IEDs will be on the same circuit. There will likely be a battery pack somewhere, but we're going to presume that will be too difficult to access. The targets are probably keeping watch on it anyway. Your best bet is to cut a main cable. Can you see two cables circling the room? One of them is the main cable. The other will have spurs leading off to each individual device. You need to identify the right one, then cut it using the blade hidden in the heel of your shoe.

Again Max didn't reply. The Chinese girl was still watching him. Why was she doing that? Why couldn't she just look in the other direction? Max glanced at the cables circling the room. Angel was right: there were two. One was red, the other black. From his position at the back of the hall, he couldn't tell which was the main cable and which was the spur cable. He tried to look over the heads of the crouching kids blocking his view but it was no good. He would have to get closer.

He looked at the stage. The others were still in the same position, under surveillance by T1. They could do nothing to help. If he stood up and walked towards one of the devices, he'd instantly attract attention. And to remove the blade from his heel in full view of everyone would be reckless. He needed a plan. He glanced in the direction of the toilet block. There was nobody queuing right now, but Max was faintly aware that a couple of kids had just gone in. He raised a hand. T6 approached him. 'What?' he demanded in a low, harsh voice.

'I need to go,' Max said, pointing at the toilet door.

The gunman pulled him to his feet, gripping his arm hard with strong, gloved hands. 'Wait outside,' he said. He pushed him towards the door. Max almost tripped over a couple of other kids. He winced – his ankle was still a little sore from the paracord incident – but regained his footing and waited outside the toilet door.

He felt as if everyone in the hall was watching him. He

wasn't far wrong. The other recruits were looking in his direction, and he didn't dare catch their eyes. But he'd caused a disturbance when he stood up. Now most of the hostages and even the targets and decoys were looking his way. He cursed silently. How could he examine the cables when everybody was watching him?

It was the Chinese girl who helped him out, even though she didn't mean to. Max had become used to the low-level noise of little kids crying. He had started to block it out. But one child was making more noise than the others. He was sitting close to where Jack lay in front of the stage. The little boy was sobbing noisily and uncontrollably. As Max looked across the heads of the other hostages, he could see why. A gruesome trickle of blood was flowing from Jack's nose. His face was white. He looked like a corpse.

The sight chilled Max, but he was distracted by the Chinese girl striding up to the wailing kid. She pulled him roughly to his feet and started hissing something at him. Then she clipped him hard round the back of the head.

One of the teachers dressed as a decoy reacted immediately. From her – she looked female to Max – position by the blacked-out window, she lurched towards the little boy. He was crying even louder now, and the Chinese girl was hissing even more intensely at him, like an angry goose.

'Get back!' T1 barked. 'Get back *now*! Or somebody will get shot!'

The teacher stopped. She spun round helplessly. T14 strode up to her and dragged her back to her original position by the window.

'Take that child to the back of the room!' T1 instructed the Chinese girl. She did as she was told, roughly pulling the crying kid away from the sight that he found so upsetting. It was clear that she was not doing it because she felt sorry for him. An unpleasant, self-satisfied smile played across her lips.

This gave Max the opportunity to examine the cables. From his position outside the toilet door, he could see the nearest IED. It was by the wall, a few metres away. He saw that the red cable snaked into the IED and emerged on the other side. The black cable continued in a circuit around the room. That meant the black cable was the one he needed to cut.

He felt a surge of anxiety. What if Angel had got it wrong, and cutting the cable triggered a detonation? His mouth went dry at the thought. But then a memory hit him: Angel, controlling the chopper in the wild blizzard above Valley House. She was calm, capable and borderline scary, but above all she knew what she was doing.

The toilet door opened. A frightened-looking boy with wonky glasses exited, accompanied by one of the targets: T7, the smallest, who seemed to have taken over this duty from T16. The boy scurried back to his group. The target turned to Max and made a 'get inside' gesture. Max made a show of meekly obeying. As he passed the target, however, he scanned what he could see of his face. Only his eyes and mouth were visible behind the balaclava, but they told him a lot. The target had a cleft lip, and there was an uncertain look in his eyes. It occurred to Max that letting kids in and out of the toilet was the worst job available to the terrorists. That meant this guy, along with T16, was bottom of the ladder.

He remembered Angel's advice. *If you can, form a rapport with them. Talk about your family – real or invented. Talk about your hobbies and your life outside the siege. Don't allow them to dehumanise you. It won't work on all of them, but there's often a weak link somewhere in the terrorist team. You might be able to use that to your advantage.*

Weak link? If there was one, maybe this guy was it.

The toilet door closed behind them. They were in a locker room, with lines of dented metal lockers and pegs. There were three doors. One led to the girls' toilets. One led to the boys'. The third was the locked door through which they had tried and failed to enter. Max headed to the boys', but then stopped to look at his new companion. 'You, er . . . you look like my brother,' he said, aware that he sounded very nervous. The idea had just dropped into his head. He pointed to his own lips. 'He has that thing you have.'

T7 stared at him through the balaclava. His eyes had widened slightly. Max had his captor's attention. Something told him nobody had ever talked kindly about his appearance before. He even felt a pang of sympathy for him . . .

He heard Hector's voice in his head. *Watch out for the signs of Stockholm Syndrome in yourselves. It's a very real thing. If you start feeling sympathy for any of these terrorists, remember: these people woke up this morning intending to kill children.*

'I got in trouble the other day,' Max continued. 'Some boys were giving my brother a hard time. I got in a fight with them.' He shrugged. 'They won't mess with my brother again, anyway.' He smiled and stepped towards the boys' toilet.

'What is your brother's name?'

'Bruce,' Max said. It was the first name that came to him. 'He had a sore throat when he woke up today, so he couldn't come to school.'

T7 looked momentarily at the floor. 'I have brother too,' he said in broken English. 'Back in Chechnya.'

Max looked at the target. 'Do you want to see your brother again?'

T7 looked away again.

'I think you do,' Max said quietly. 'I want to see mine too. I . . . I think you can help me make that happen. I don't think you're like the others.' And that, Max realised, was the truth. There was something different about this one. 'We will see our brothers again, won't we?'

The target's eyes narrowed. Did he know he was being played? He pointed at the boys' toilets. 'Go,' he said. He crossed his arms to show the conversation was at an end.

Max headed towards the boys' toilets. But then he turned back. 'If I get out of here, I'll tell them you're not like the others,' he said. Then he entered the toilet alone.

– *That was good.*

Hector sounded almost proud. Max didn't reply. Not yet. He wanted to make sure he was alone. There were six urinals and five cubicles. A line of washbasins. No windows. Three of the cubicles had closed doors. Max checked the gap at the bottom of each door to ensure nobody else was in here. Only then did he speak. 'I've identified the wire,' he said. 'I've come to the toilets to remove my razor blade. But I don't know how I'm going to cut the wire without anyone seeing. You said earlier you can create a distraction. Can you do that now?'

– *Negative. We've had to change our strategy. If we're right and the targets intend to detonate, we can't risk doing anything that will encourage them to do so. You'll have to do it covertly.*

'Great,' Max whispered. 'Just eight terrorists and two hundred and fifty hostages to worry about . . . Are you sure I'm going to be cutting the right wire? I'm not going to lie – physics was never my strong point.'

It was Angel who answered.

– *Not going to lie, hun: I aced it.*

Max chose the leftmost cubicle and locked himself inside. He closed the toilet seat and sat on it, then took off his left shoe. He unclicked the heel and removed the razor, leaving the button compass inside. He gently slid the razor blade into the back pocket of his jeans. Clicking the heel shut again, he put the shoe back on. Then he stood up, flushed the toilet, and exited the cubicle. As he headed to the door, he caught sight of himself in the mirror above the washbasins. He was shocked by how pale his face was, and by the dark rings under his eyes. He ran a cold tap and splashed some water on his face. Then he dried his face. It wasn't much, but it gave him a little bit more confidence.

'I'm heading back out,' he said into the comms.

– *Roger that.*

He tried to think of something he could say to the target waiting outside. Something to make him seem more like a human being, less like a victim. Maybe he'd ask him about the rest of his family, he thought. It would make more of a bond between them. He found himself thinking of questions in his head as he stepped out of the boys' toilets and into the locker room. *Do you have any sisters? Where do your mum and dad live? Do they know . . .*

He stopped stock-still.

There was no sign of T7 in the locker room. But it wasn't deserted. The Chinese girl stood to one side of the door. Her arms were crossed. One eyebrow was raised. Her expression was hard.

'What were you doing in there?' she said.

17

Lightning Fast

'The usual,' Max replied.

He didn't want to get into a conversation with this girl, so he headed straight for the door.

She moved quicker than Max had ever seen anybody move. Her right arm blocked the doorway. With her left arm, she grabbed him by the shoulder. Her grip was strong.

'You're fast,' Max breathed.

'Lightning fast,' the girl said. 'And expert in four martial arts. I can break your arm in two seconds and both your legs in three. You're not leaving this room until we've finished talking.'

'There's nothing to talk about,' Max said. 'I need to get back out there. They'll wonder what I'm doing in here. I don't want to make them angry.' The razor blade in his back pocket suddenly felt ten times larger and heavier.

'You're not from this school,' the girl said.

Max tried not to show any emotion. 'Course I am,' he said. 'Why else would I be here?'

She stepped forward. 'You are not. Nor are the people up on the stage. I have a photographic memory.'

'You're quite the superwoman,' Max muttered.

'I've been here for a week and I recognise *everybody*. You are not from this school. You arrived after the siege started.'

Max said nothing.

The Chinese girl looked over her shoulder at the closed door. Then back at Max. Her hard exterior seemed to soften. She released her grip on him. 'We don't have much time,' she said, very quietly. 'You must disable those devices quickly.'

Max narrowed his eyes at her. 'What do you mean?' he said.

– *Watch out. She might be trying to trick you.*

The girl rolled her eyes. 'Look, it's obvious, isn't it? You five arrived long after the siege began. You must have been sent in by someone on the outside. Your friends are either being watched or they're . . .' She let that sentence trail away. Max wondered if she was thinking about Jack. 'You're the only one with a chance of doing anything. I saw you looking at the cables and the explosive devices when I distracted the terrorists by talking to the crying boy. So you must be thinking of disabling them.'

– *Don't admit anything. Let her keep talking.*

'You have to do it quickly,' the Chinese girl said. 'I heard two of them talking before you arrived. They're not going to let the siege go on much longer. They're waiting for a rescue team to come so they can kill some soldiers as well as us. But if it doesn't arrive by two o'clock, they're going to detonate the devices anyway.'

Max looked at his watch. It was half past one. He looked back at the girl. 'Are you telling me you speak Chechen, on top of everything else?'

'Russian,' she replied immediately. 'They were talking in Russian and I do speak that. And English, Mandarin and Arabic.'

'How come?'

'Does it matter? Languages are my thing.'

'Is there anything you can't do?'

'Yes. Cook.' She didn't even look like she was joking.

'What's your name?' he asked.

'Lili. Listen, there are other things you need to know. You noticed the people with guns taped to their arms?'

Max didn't want to give anything away. 'Go on,' he said.

'There are eight of them. Seven of them are teachers. But one of them is a terrorist.'

'Which one?'

'I don't know.' She shook her head desperately. 'I've been trying to work it out, but they're all dressed the same. The teachers' guns are empty, but his one is loaded.' She fixed Max with a sincere look. 'You have to believe me. It's the terrorists I was deceiving. I'm telling you the truth.'

There was a moment of silence. Then Max heard Abby's voice in his ear.

– She's lying. You saw her in here. She's totally lying.

Max remained expressionless. The next voice he heard was Angel's.

– You're going to have to make this call, Max. You're the one talking to her. Only you can decide. Is she lying or telling the truth? Go with your gut instinct.

He stared at Lili. She was a different person to the one he'd seen in the hall. She seemed smaller. Less aggressive. And frightened.

'There's another thing,' Lili said. 'Those vests some of them are wearing – they have a special kind of detonator. I heard them calling it a kill switch. I think it means that once they press the switch with their thumb, the vest is primed. As soon as the switch is released, the vest detonates. So, as soon as the switch has been pressed . . .'

'. . . if the target gets shot, the vest explodes.' Max finished the sentence for her.

'Right,' Lili said. She looked even more frightened now. Nobody could fake that kind of fear. Max knew, because he felt it too.

'She's telling the truth,' Max said quietly.

Lili looked confused. 'Who are you talking to?'

'It doesn't matter.' He took a deep breath, then went for it. 'I need to cut one of the cables circling the room. Can you help me by distracting the terrorists?'

Lili looked thoughtful. 'I can do better than that,' she said after a moment. 'But we have to move fast.'

166

'Right,' Max said. He managed a smile. 'Lightning fast.'

Lili nodded seriously. She looked as though she was about to explain her plan. Just then, however, the door opened. T7 appeared. He looked from Lili to Max and back again. Her features morphed. The other Lili – hard-faced, aggressive and a bit scary – reappeared. 'Get back in there,' she said, her voice loud enough to be heard back in the hall. 'Now!'

Max bowed his head and did as he was told. As he entered the hall followed by Lili and T7, Lili pushed officiously past him. She strode across the hall towards T1, who was still on the stage. Max watched as she had a hushed conversation with him. So did everyone else in the hall. Lili pointed at Jack, who was still unconscious on the ground in front of the stage. T1 nodded. Lili walked off the stage and stood beside Jack. She scanned everyone in the room. Max was still standing up, and she pointed at him. 'You!' she called out across the hall. 'Come here.'

The room fell silent. Max felt all eyes on him as he picked his way across the hall. When he reached Lili, he looked down at Jack. Max was shocked. Jack's face was pale, bruised and smeared with blood. His right arm looked broken, bent at a strange angle at the elbow. Max looked for the faint rising and falling of his chest. He couldn't see it. He glanced up at the others on the stage. They were watching intently. Abby's mistrust of Lili was plain to read on her face.

'The sight of this idiot is upsetting the small children,' Lili said. 'You must help me move him.' She walked round to Jack's feet. 'I will take this end, you take the head end. We will move him to the back of the room.'

Max didn't understand what she was doing, but did as he was told. Not knowing if he was dealing with a corpse or a live body, he lifted Jack beneath the shoulders, taking care not to move his broken arm any more than was necessary. Jack was heavier than he looked. It took him and Lili a couple of attempts to get him off the ground. The kids nearby shuffled across the floor to open up a path towards the back of the dining hall. Lili avoided Max's gaze as they carried Jack to the back of the hall. After a moment, the general low hubbub returned. 'Put him right against the back wall,' Lili said, loud enough for only Max to hear. 'We can place him so that he covers the cable. That way, they won't see that you've cut it.'

Max had to hand it to her: it was a good idea. At the back of the hall, they laid Jack on the ground so there was only a tiny gap between him and the back wall. Lili stood directly in front of Max, who was still crouching down over Jack. Max understood why: it gave him a moment of camouflage to pull the razor from his back pocket without anybody else seeing.

He pulled out the razor and concealed it in his palm. He could sense Lili walking away from him. He continued to lean over Jack, as if tending to him. He put one finger on his neck and pressed lightly against the jugular, feeling for a pulse. It was weak, but it was there. Relief flooded over him. Jack was alive. Barely, maybe, but alive. With his other hand he reached behind the unconscious recruit. He grabbed the two cables, one black and one red. He felt the nape of his neck tingling, as though somebody was watching him. But he knew that was just his anxiety. This was his best chance to cut the cable.

He let the red cable fall and rested the sharp edge of the razor blade against the black cable. He half expected his hands to be trembling, but they were not. All he could do was hope Angel had given him the right information and this was indeed the cable he needed to cut.

'Now or never,' he muttered to himself.

He sliced the cable in two.

Nothing happened.

That was good. He didn't know for sure that he had disabled the IEDs, but at least he hadn't detonated them. He placed the two ends of the severed cable behind Jack. He made a show of checking Jack's pulse again. He hoped the unconscious recruit was going to be okay. But he also hoped he didn't wake up too soon and try to move.

'We'll get you out of here, mate,' he breathed. 'I promise . . .'

– *What's happening?*

'It's cut,' Max breathed. He turned round. He remained on the floor, hugging his knees as he surveyed what was

169

going on in the room. Lili had resumed her officious patrol. It was plain that the younger children were frightened of her and the way that she was apparently siding with the terrorists. They seemed to shrink away whenever she came close. The older kids looked contemptuous of her, but they didn't say or do anything to make her notice them. The other recruits were still kneeling on the stage. Abby had a distant but steely look on her face, like she was preparing herself for something. Sami was staring up at the far wall. Max assumed he was looking at the clock as it ticked its way towards 14:00. It was Lukas who caught Max's eye. There was something in that brief look. It was an expression of support, confidence and respect. Was there an apology there too? Max wasn't sure, but it meant a lot to him anyway, even though he didn't dare acknowledge it. T11 was patrolling close to him.

Most alarming, though, was the behaviour of the terrorists. T1 had stepped down from the stage. He shouted something in a foreign language. The seven other targets joined him and stood in a ring. A nervous hush fell on the hall as they discussed something in low voices. It took no longer than thirty seconds. They each made a strange gesture, something between a handshake and a fist bump.

Max checked his watch. It was 13:45.

Fifteen minutes until 14:00.

He felt his blood go cold. 'They're getting ready,' he

said quietly. He was able to speak because the terrorists were focused entirely on themselves for a moment.

– *Wait*. Hector's voice was emotionless.

Max didn't get a chance to reply. His attention was on Lili. She was standing at the front of the hall, staring officiously over the heads of the hostages. Was she trying to avoid catching his eye? Max wondered.

T1 stood behind her. 'You,' he said harshly, 'get down.'

Lili turned. 'What do you mean?' she said. 'I've been helping you. You said you would release me first.'

'Nobody gets released,' said T1. 'Get down.' He raised his fist as if to strike her. Lili fell to the ground. Lukas, Abby and Sami watched her in horror. Just like Max, they surely knew what this meant. If the terrorists were silencing Lili, their supposed helper, it meant they were definitely approaching their endgame.

'We *have* to do something . . .' he breathed.

– *Wait.*

'We can't wait! It's about to happen! They got into a kind of huddle, like they were giving each other confidence to do something big. They've forced Lili onto the ground . . .'

– *Keep cool, Max. You're no use to anybody if you're panicking.*

Max inhaled deeply in an attempt to slow down his racing pulse. 'They . . . they look like they're getting into position . . . I think they're going to detonate their suicide vests. I think Lili was right. She said they were going to do it at 14:00. if there was no rescue attempt by then. We've only got fifteen minutes.'

And when there was no reply, he spoke as forcefully as he dared. 'Can you hear me? How am I supposed to keep cool when we've only got fifteen minutes before this whole place blows and we go with it?'

18

State Your Name

The targets turned.

They looked around the room.

Then they started to spread out.

Four of them moved up onto the stage, where they stood behind the recruits, spaced out. The remaining four lined up alongside the blind-covered windows. They positioned themselves in between the teachers, facing inwards with their backs to the window. Max had lost track of who was who. All he knew was that T1 was on the stage and T7 by the south window. T1 had something in his hands: a black box with a flick switch. Max realised what it must be: a remote detonator for the IEDs. His mouth turned dry as he worried once more whether he'd cut the right cable.

'They're putting themselves into position!' he said, louder than he intended. One of the decoys looked over at him. So did a few nearby kids. Max rested his head against his knees, as if in desperation.

Hector's voice finally burst once more over the comms.

– *That's what we want them to do, Max. Are some of them standing by the windows?*

'Yes,' Max hissed.

– *That's because they want the explosion to be spectacular, when it happens, for the press cameras. Blowing out the windows is the best way to do that. Now listen carefully. We have SAS personnel moving onto target. There is a four-man unit currently in hiding underneath the stage.*

'What?' Max breathed, lowering his head so he couldn't be seen talking. 'How did they get there? I didn't hear them.'

– *Of course you didn't hear them. They're the SAS. They gained access via the sewer system. We also have two sniper teams on the perimeter of the school and on the roof of Block Red. They have rifles trained on the two long windows of the hall.*

'But they can't see through them. The blinds are down . . .'

– *That's where you come in. Remember, we can see shadows through the blinds. Are you able to see all the targets?*

He looked around the hall again. There were four targets at the back of the stage. Two along one wall, two along the other, mixed up with the decoy teachers. 'Er . . . I think so.'

– *The north wall, to the left of the stage as you look*

at it, is wall A. The south wall is wall B. The west wall leading to the kitchen is wall C. State the positions of the targets in reference to the stage and walls A, B and C. And make it accurate, Max. We don't want to put bullets in the wrong people.

Max swallowed hard. He kept his head low so that nobody could see him moving his mouth. But his eyes picked out the targets one by one.

'There are four targets at the back of the stage,' he whispered, 'and two each along wall A and wall B. There are no targets on wall C.'

– That's good. I want you to concentrate on the targets along wall A. We can detect the shadows of six figures. They look like adults. From what you've told us, that's four decoys and two actual targets. Cough once if we've got that wrong, otherwise keep quiet.

Max kept quiet.

– Counting from the stage end to the back of the hall, I want you to give each figure a number from one to six. Cough when I say the number that corresponds to the two real targets. One. Two.

Max coughed.

– Three. Four. Five.

He coughed again.

– Six. My information is that the real targets are figures two and five, moving from the stage backwards. Cough if that is correct.

He coughed again. The kid sitting nearby with the ginger hair gave him a strange look. 'Asthma,' Max told him quietly, and the kid looked away.

There was a moment of silence. Max felt that the panic in the hall had increased. It was clear everyone knew something was about to happen. The hum of voices had grown a little louder. T1 shouted from the back of the stage: 'Quiet!' It had no immediate effect. T1 engaged his weapon and stepped to the front of the stage. He put his weapon against the back of Sami's head. '*QUIET!*' he roared. Sami closed his eyes. The hall fell silent. The gunman kept his weapon to the back of the Sami's skull for a full twenty seconds, before returning to his position at the back of the stage.

Max checked his watch. 13:51. Nine minutes to go. 'We need to do something,' he breathed. When Hector spoke again over the comms, it was with a renewed sense of urgency.

– *We're going to turn our attention to wall B. Same drill, from the stage backwards. One.*

Cough.

– *Two. Three. Four.*

Cough.

– *Five. Six. My information is that the two targets along wall B are in positions one and four. Cough if that's correct.*

Max coughed again.

– If any of the targets move from their current positions, you need to tell me.

A pause. More kids were crying. Panic was rising again. But the targets remained in position. Max glanced at T7. Of all the targets, he was closest to Max. He seemed to be muttering something to himself. And while the other targets seemed pumped up, T7's shoulders were slumped. His body was somehow different. For a moment, Max doubted that he truly had the courage to go through with this.

And talking of courage . . .

Max checked his watch. 13:56. They had four minutes. He could feel his blood pumping in his veins. When he heard Hector's voice again, he started so violently that a couple of the nearby kids gave him a sharp look, despite their own obvious fear.

– This is what's going to happen. When I give the word, Lukas, Abby and Sami must jump off the stage, leaving only four targets on the stage. The sniper teams will take shots at the window targets. Simultaneously, there will be an explosion beneath the stage and the team below will take out the targets on stage. That will neutralise all targets except one: the fake decoy. From what you say, he's the only target without a suicide vest, but his weapon is probably loaded.

Time check: 13:57.

T1 looked at his watch, then stared straight ahead. T7

was still mumbling to himself. He caught Max's eye and cocked his head strangely. Max looked away.

– *We don't know who the fake decoy is, so you're going to have to move fast. There will be confusion, smoke and noise. There will be bright lights and loud bangs as the SAS team detonate flashbang grenades. This is to make the environment so confusing that the remaining target is too disorientated to harm the hostages. But we will have limited time to identify him or her. You must go through the room, demanding the decoys' names. We will be able to hear their responses over the comms. If they give a correct name, we'll tell you. Make them lie on their front with their hands on their heads. If you find a decoy who cannot answer the question correctly, you must do everything you can to overwhelm him or her. Get him on the ground and shout 'Target'. One of the SAS team will find you and do the rest.*

The words 'do the rest' had an awful note of finality about them. Max swallowed hard. He checked his watch again.

13:58.

They had two minutes. Maybe less.

– *Are the targets still in position? Cough once for yes.*

Cough.

– *Then prepare for the strike. Assault team, stand by. Sniper teams, stand by. Lukas, Abby, Sami, get ready to jump. We are a go in three . . .*

Maybe it had been a premonition. Maybe something Max had said had touched him. But in the fraction of a second before the order was given, T7 looked in his direction.

– Two . . .

Max remembered his words in the locker room – *I have brother too. Back in Chechnya* – and felt a momentary pang of sympathy.

– One . . .

Max's eyes flickered anxiously towards the window behind T7's head. T7 seemed to notice this. He cocked his head and threw himself to the ground.

– Go go go!

Everything seemed to happen at the same time. Lukas, Abby and Sami jumped to their feet and hurled themselves off the stage. There were shouts of alarm from the hostages. A fraction of a second later, there was an enormous explosion from the back of the stage and a flash of blinding light. It sent a physical jolt through Max's body, as though somebody had pushed him hard. There was the distant retort of weapons, and the splintering of broken glass as the windows imploded. The blinds were breached on both sides of the hall by incoming sniper rounds. They were aimed precisely at the four targets that Max had identified. But only three had still been in place.

Out of the corner of his eye, Max was aware of gruesome explosions of blood and brain matter as three targets collapsed to the ground. Screams ripped through the air. Groups of hostages fled from the horrific sight of the bleeding corpses. Max's attention, though, was all on the target who had *not* been hit by the sniper round intended for him. His attention was on T7.

The loose sniper round had slammed into the floor of the dining hall, just missing a child. More people started shouting in panic. The atmosphere in the room had deteriorated into panic. For Max, however, the voices of the other hostages receded in comparison to the commotion at the back of the stage. He looked up to see that it had collapsed in a billowing cloud of smoke. There was no sign of the targets who had been standing there, but it was immediately clear what their fate was: Max heard a sequence of four double shots as the hidden SAS team dealt with them, terminally.

So far, the assault had lasted less than five seconds. Already seven targets were dead.

That left two: T7, and the fake decoy.

Max was astonished by how quickly the smoke billowed out from the back of the stage. In an instant, the air in the hall was thick and choking. He could hardly breathe and couldn't see more than a metre in front of him. He found himself shouting, 'Seven targets down! Two targets remaining! One of them has a vest!'

For the first time there was a note of panic in Hector's voice.

– *FIND HIM. PUT HIM DOWN! REPEAT: PUT . . . HIM . . . DOWN!*

Max jumped to his feet and spun round. There was such panic and chaos all around him. Kids yelling. Bodies pushing up against each other. He held his breath to stop the dust in the air getting into his lungs. He heard Lukas's voice in his ear.

– *Me and Abby are searching the north side. Sami and Max, take the south.*

It was a good plan. 'Roger that,' Max agreed. He surged towards the south window of the hall. Almost immediately, he encountered a decoy. 'State your name!' he shouted over the deafening noise of and panic. '*Tell me your name, now!*'

The decoy did as she was told. 'S-Sandra Wilkinson . . .'

Hector immediately gave an instruction over the comms.

– *Confirmed. She's a teacher. Get her on the ground.*

'Lie on your front with your hands on the back of your head!' Max shouted at her. 'Do it now or they'll shoot you!'

The teacher didn't need telling twice. She fell to the ground as if she had been shot. Over his comms earpiece, Max heard three other teachers being identified by Lukas, Abby and Sami.

– *Helen Wilcox.*

– Confirmed.

– Get on the ground!

– Jeremy Wood.

– Confirmed.

– Get down, now, or they'll shoot!

– Ali McGuigan.

– Confirmed.

– Get on the ground, hands behind your head!

Max moved along the window towards the stage, feeling his way through the smoke. He felt something slippery underfoot. Looking down, he realised it was blood, oozing from the head of one of the targets who had been shot. He retched but kept moving. Five seconds later, he encountered another decoy. 'State your name!'

The decoy said something but her words were lost as Lukas shouted over the comms.

– State your name!

No reply.

– STATE YOUR NAME!

Max's decoy whispered something.

'Alexandra Marriott.'

As Hector confirmed that she was a genuine teacher, Max pushed her to the ground and spun round. The dust was clearing somewhat. The hostages were all crowding at the back of the hall, away from the stage, though some of the younger ones, too terrified to move, were still huddled in the middle of the hall. Through watering eyes, Max could see Lukas clutching one of the decoys by the front of their overalls. The decoy was taller and broader than Lukas. He was kicking out. But Lukas, smaller though he was, was plainly stronger. He had the decoy on the ground in seconds, and was ripping off his balaclava.

To Max's right was the stage, demolished by the explosion. Emerging from the rubble, however, were four figures. Max could tell that they were not terrorists. They were dressed in camouflage gear, with military helmets, protective goggles and respirator masks. They wore heavy tactical vests and backpacks with antennae pointing out. And they carried assault rifles, the butts pressed into their shoulders, the barrels scanning the room as the gunmen searched the chaos for targets. Red laser sights cut through the smoke. The SAS had arrived. They looked like killing machines.

Max couldn't see Abby or Sami, but he could hear them. Over comms they were identifying two more teachers. It meant all the genuine teachers were accounted for. Lukas's guy had to be the fake decoy. He had to be a target.

'It's him!' Lukas shouted. Max could hear his voice, both over the comms and in real life. He could also see two members of the SAS peel away from the others and sprint towards where Lukas had pinned the target to the ground. As the soldiers closed in on him, the target started to struggle more violently. Lukas was holding down his right hand to stop him activating his kill switch, but that meant the terrorist could fight back more easily with the rest of his body. It almost looked as if he might overcome Lukas. But the SAS men were close now . . .

Max turned his head. He knew what they would do, and he had no desire to witness it. As he focused on the rest of the hall, he heard the suppressed thud of two rifle rounds in quick succession. He knew the decoy target did not pose a problem any more.

But T7 did. He was still alive, his suicide vest still active. He was somewhere in the hall. If he had activated his kill switch, he could detonate himself at any moment.

Max looked around. Surely his only sensible move was to find cover. To save himself from the explosion he knew must be seconds away. He couldn't head to the kitchen exit – too many people crowded round it. His eyes fell on the demolished stage. If he ran there, he could take cover in the rubble. Like Sami, hiding under the pile of bricks on day one of selection. That was his best chance of survival. He took a step towards it . . .

But then Hector's voice rang in his head. *I knew your dad . . . He was always the first man in and the last man out . . . Brave to a fault.. What would he think if he knew that you were considering giving up now, when so many people's lives are at risk, and they all depend on you?*

Max halted. He looked over at the child hostages crowding round the exit. T7 had to be among them, on the point of detonating his suicide vest.

Somehow, he had to be stopped.

19

Kill Switch

Max flung himself towards the crowd of hostages, convinced he was the only one who could stop the impending carnage. He had looked into T7's eyes. There had been uncertainty in his look. If Max could get in front of him again, maybe he could talk the final target into disarming himself. Or at least delay the inevitable while he tried to come up with something better.

A scream pierced the noise in the hall. As Max ran at the crowd, it parted in front of him. 'Get down!' an adult voice shouted from behind him. 'Everyone get down and cover your heads!' A few of the child hostages followed his instruction. Others turned to look at who was shouting. The piercing scream had come from a young child with albino-white hair. As the space ahead of Max opened out, he saw what had frightened the kid so much.

It frightened Max too.

Through the settling dust he saw Lili. She was in a space, on her knees, back straight, head high, arms by her side. Behind her was T7. In his left hand was a handgun.

It was pressed into the back of Lili's skull. In his right hand was a cylindrical object, no bigger than a ballpoint pen. It had a button on the top. T7 had pressed it down with his thumb.

The kill switch was activated.

From the corner of his eye, Max saw the awesome figures of the SAS men. 'Don't fire!' he shouted, unsure whether they were patched into his comms. 'He's got a kill switch. It's activated. If you shoot him, it'll blow.'

Max's voice echoed around the hall. The child hostages had fallen silent. He felt all their eyes on him, but Max's attention was firmly on T7.

The target was shaking violently. He was clearly as scared as everybody else. He held the kill switch aloft – a threat to everyone in the room. But he hadn't detonated it. Did that mean he wasn't ready to die yet? Max didn't know.

Max held up both hands, palms outward, to show he was unarmed. 'It's me,' he said. 'Remember me?'

T7 didn't speak, but he nodded his head almost imperceptibly.

'I meant it when I said I'd tell them about you not being like the others,' Max said. 'You're not, are you? You don't want to die, like them, do you?'

In his peripheral vision, Max saw Lukas, Abby and Sami approaching. They were carrying weapons and he assumed that they'd taken them from the dead targets.

'Stand back, everyone,' Max said. 'Lower your weapons. I know this guy. He's not like the others. He doesn't want to do this. Do you, mate?' He smiled at T7. 'You want to see your brother again, right? And he wants to see you.'

T7 licked his dry lips nervously. He gave another very faint nod. It gave Max hope.

Max looked around the room. Lukas, Abby and Sami had lowered their weapons. The SAS men – two of them behind T7, two of them behind Max – had not. Their weapons were trained on T7's head.

'Seriously, guys,' Max said in a level voice. 'Lower them. If you shoot him, we all die. He knows that.'

There was a ten-second pause. Then, very slowly, the SAS men lowered their weapons.

'I'm going to take a step forward,' Max said. 'You good with that?' He started to step forward.

Something changed.

'No!' T7 barked.

Max froze. He saw that T7's trembling had increased. In a flash of sudden insight he realised that his hope was misplaced. T7 was backed into a corner. He was scared. But when he came down to it, he had no real option. He wouldn't be talked round. He'd woken up that morning knowing he was going to die, and that's what he intended to do.

He was going to detonate.

Everyone in the vicinity would die.

Unless Max could come up with something.

Max took a step back and glanced at Lili. Considering the danger she was in, she appeared incredibly calm. He looked back at T7.

'Nobody's going to get too close to you,' he said quietly. 'That's a kill switch in your right hand and a semi-automatic in your left. We get it. We understand that all you have to do is lift your right thumb and we all die.' He hoped Lili was listening. 'We understand you're in charge.'

'I *am* in charge,' T7 said. His voice was hoarse, and it shook.

'Nobody can stop you,' Max agreed. 'They'd have to be . . .' His eyes flickered to Lili again. 'They'd have to be lightning fast.'

– *What are you doing, Max? What's going on?* Hector was even more abrupt than usual. He even sounded scared.

But there was no time to explain. A flicker of a smile crossed Lili's lips. She clearly understood what Max was trying to tell her. He had given her all the information she needed. Their survival was up to her now.

Everything happened so quickly. T7's eyes rolled. He drew back his shoulders as though preparing for something. Lili closed her eyes for the briefest moment, as though she was drawing strength from another place. Then her hands shot up. With her left hand she grabbed the weapon that was pressed into the back of her head and pushed it away. Her other hand grabbed T7's right fist and closed over it, pressing his thumb down on to the kill switch so he couldn't release it.

A wild look crossed T7's face. He fired. The retort echoed around the hall. Many of the hostages screamed as the round slammed into the overhead lighting and a shower of glass and sparks rained down on the wooden floor. Lili's face was a picture of concentration as she used every scrap of strength she had to keep the kill switch down and the weapon pointing out of harm's way. Max dived at her, and he was aware of Lukas, Sami and Abby sprinting to his aid.

He added his strength to Lili's by grabbing T7's gun hand. His eyes scanned the dull grey firearm and he quickly identified the safety switch. With his free hand he clicked the gun safe. 'Get him on the ground!' he shouted. 'Three, two, one . . .'

It was as if he and Lili were one person. Just as Max hooked one leg round T7's ankle, he felt Lili pulling him to the ground, her right hand still keeping the kill switch depressed. T7 collapsed with a thump. As he did, the other recruits were there. Abby crouched by Lili and lent her strength to the crucial task of maintaining pressure on T7's thumb. Lukas tore the pistol from T7's hand, de-cocking it and removing the magazine before sitting on T7's kicking legs.

Sami did not join them. He was still carrying one of the

terrorists' MP5s. He brandished it with the light-handed skill of a weapons expert. And he circled round the target, aiming the gun not at T7 but at the SAS men who were closing in, their weapons fully engaged. They were pointing at a downward angle, towards T7. With a sick feeling, Max realised they were moving in for the kill.

'Put the weapon down, son!' one of them shouted.

'No!' Sami shouted. 'You put down *your* weapons. You don't need to use them!'

– *What's happening? Sami, what are you doing?*

'Get down!' barked another of the SAS men. 'Lower that weapon.'

But Sami was clearly in no mood to be talked down. 'He's under control! You don't need to shoot him! Enough people have died!'

Max remembered what Hector had told them about Sami. *He spent those nine months with an AK-47 in his hand, protecting his family from people who wanted to kill them. I don't know how many government troops he was forced to shoot. I'll never ask him, and I hope none of you do either, when you get out of here.*

It made sense to Max why Sami didn't want to see any more killing. But it didn't make sense to the SAS man. 'Get down!' the same guy repeated.

Hostages were escaping from the hall through the kitchen. The main doors to the right of the south window burst open. More military personnel sprinted in. Max saw

Hector, Woody and Angel, their eyes burning, their hair dishevelled. But they hung back as two men in helmets and protective clothing sprinted up to the recruits who were pinning T7 to the ground. One of them carried a square box on his back with two antennae – Max knew that this was a mobile phone jammer, in case anyone was using a phone to detonate any devices – but neither appeared to be armed. 'EOD – Explosive Ordnance Disposal! Keep that kill switch down!'

One of the EOD guys knelt down and leaned over T7, who was struggling harder than ever. It took all of Max's strength to hold him down as the EOD guy removed wire cutters and traced one finger along the cables spewing from T7's vest. He was clearly deciding which one to cut. The SAS men were closing in now, not on T7 but on Sami, whose face was sweating.

'Lower your weapon!' one of the SAS men shouted.

Still Sami refused. For a dreadful moment, Max thought the SAS team would open fire. But then he heard Hector bellowing across the hall. 'Assault team, stand down! Assault team, stand down! That's an order.'

The SAS men looked uncertainly at each other, but they followed the instruction and lowered their weapons. At the same time, the EOD guy shouted, 'We're clear! The device is neutralised. It's safe to release the kill switch.'

Only then did Sami lower his weapon. He was breathing

heavily and his shoulders were shaking. Max turned his attention to Abby and Lili. They were looking anxiously at each other. 'You sure?' Abby asked. 'Now's not a good time to make a mistake . . .'

The EOD man held up a wire leading from T7's vest. 'It's disconnected,' he said. 'Trust me.'

Abby inclined her head, then nodded at Lili. Together they released the kill switch. Nothing happened.

Max exhaled slowly. He released T7's arm. The terrorist had gone limp, as if all the fight had left him. Max moved his hand up to the terrorist's balaclava. T7 didn't fight when Max peeled it from his face.

T7 was young. Not much older than Max himself. There was a whisper of unshaved hair on his chin and cheeks. He was very pale.

Max became aware of Sami standing over them. 'I hope you see your brother again,' Max said quietly. 'If you do, it's him you have to thank.' He pointed up at Sami.

T7 looked at them. A sneer crossed his face. He spat at Max.

Max stood up, shocked. One of the SAS guys pulled him and Sami back.

'That's gratitude for you,' Max said.

'It's a normal response,' the SAS man said, his voice muffled by his respirator mask. 'In his head, he's just lost a battle.'

'But he's still alive.'

'And maybe, at some point in the future, he'll be grateful for that. But right now, you're his enemy. You need to get used to that.'

'To having enemies?'

'Right. In this line of work, we collect them like other people collect stamps.'

The SAS man was called away by one of his colleagues. Max and Sami looked around the hall. The dust had settled. More EOD men were swarming over the IEDs around the room. All the hostages had left. Medics had arrived and had surrounded Jack. The decoys were being helped up by armed police and military personnel. Max averted his eyes from the dead bodies on the floor.

The SAS team roughly pulled T7 from the ground, cuffed his hands behind his back and hustled him to the exit. The recruits gathered in a group, with Lili standing slightly apart, looking unsure what to do. Hector, Woody and Angel hurried up to them. If Hector was pleased with the outcome, he didn't show it. Over the comms he'd been calm, even helpful. Now he looked like he was back to his old self.

'You!' He pointed at Sami. 'Next time a four-man SAS unit are pointing their weapons in your direction, my advice is to drop your gun.'

Sami drew himself up to his full height. 'Next time you want to kill a man who doesn't need to be killed, my advice is to make sure I'm not in the way.'

'I warned you about Stockholm Syndrome. You were weak.'

'No, I was strong. I've seen too many people die.'

Hector looked like he was thinking of a reply. None came. He turned to Woody and Angel. 'Get this lot back to Valley House,' he said. 'Now.' He turned and strode out of the hall.

Woody winked at them. 'You heard the man,' he said. 'Let's go.'

Woody and Angel followed Hector to the exit. But the recruits lagged behind. They had all turned to Lili. Max guessed that they were thinking the same as him. Without her, they'd likely all be dead.

An armed policeman approached. 'We need to get you out of here, missie,' he told Lili.

Lili blinked at him. '*Missie?*' she said incredulously. She rolled her eyes. The policeman looked embarrassed. Lili turned her back on him and awkwardly raised one hand at the recruits. 'Er . . . bye then.' The recruits nodded a farewell and watched as she was led in the direction of the door. But before she exited, she turned back to look at them. 'Who *are* you?' she said.

The recruits looked at each other. None of them knew what to say. In the end, it was Max who spoke. 'We're nobody,' he said.

Lili gave him a disbelieving smile. 'Right,' she said. 'Well, nice to meet you, nobody,' she said. 'Maybe we can do it again someday.' She looked around the room. 'On second thoughts . . .'

She followed the policeman out of the hall via the kitchen. Max, Lukas, Abby and Sami followed Woody and Angel to the main exit. The hall was still swarming with military personnel, but their work here was done.

20

Train Hard, Fight Easy

Outside the school, it was chaos. Soldiers herded the hostages out of the school grounds towards some medical tents that had been set up in the street outside. There was shouting and tears. Sirens blared. A line of police officers struggled to keep families and journalists behind the cordon. There were several ambulances. Max saw Jack being carried into one of them on a stretcher bed.

They had less than a minute to take it all in. Woody and Angel ushered them hurriedly back into the white van that had brought them here. Max sensed that they didn't want anybody on the outside to see them, or ask who they were.

The recruits wore haunted, shell-shocked expressions, as though they couldn't quite believe what had just happened. They sat silently in the van as it pulled away from the school and left the area. The seat where Jack should have been sitting was noticeably empty. Although none of them spoke, they all, at some point, glanced at that empty seat. Max knew they were all thinking the same thing: it could have been any of them being stretchered into the ambulance.

'Is he going to be okay?' Lukas asked after they had been travelling for five minutes.

Woody and Angel looked at Hector, as if expecting him to reply. When he didn't, Angel spoke. 'We don't know,' she said. 'But we don't expect him to return to Valley House.'

There was a moment of quiet as they digested that news. The others looked as shocked as Max felt.

It was Abby who broke the silence. 'So that's me, Sami and Lukas on the team,' she said. 'Our five-person team is looking kind of depleted, wouldn't you say?' When none of the Watchers replied, she said, 'If only we knew somebody else who was up to this kind of work, huh?'

They watched Hector. Were they thinking the same as Max: that he had been the most active member of their group during the siege? But if Hector intended to change his mind about him, he showed no sign of it. He stared impassively straight ahead.

'Does anybody have anything to eat?' Abby asked of nobody in particular.

Green Thunder was waiting for them at a different location: the central square of an army barracks, somewhere in the middle of London, Max didn't know where. Its rotors were already turning as they exited the transit van. Although there was no longer any urgency, the recruits and their Watchers ran up the tailgate and took their usual places. They were airborne within minutes.

A vicious tiredness overcame Max. Uncomfortable though he was, strapped into the dirty, noisy aircraft, his head started to loll. He drowsed, disturbed by dreams of masked figures and screaming children. He felt like he had only been asleep for ten minutes when he was woken by the familiar jolt of the chopper's landing gear touching the ground. His whole body ached with fatigue. It was a struggle to unclip himself, get to his feet and leave the aircraft.

It was dusk. The two sides of the valley were bathed in red light and the shadows were long. As the recruits trudged, exhausted, to their Nissen huts, Hector finally spoke. 'There will be a badging ceremony for the successful cadets on the parade ground in ten minutes. You will each receive a Special Forces Cadets challenge coin. It's a medallion bearing the SFC insignia. Keep it with you at all times. It can be hidden in a belt, a shoe or a watch and used to prove your identity, should that ever be necessary. Continuation training starts at 07:00 tomorrow. Get moving.' As Lukas, Sami and Abby continued towards their huts, he said, 'Not you, Max.'

Max watched the others go.

Hector walked up to him. 'Follow me,' he said.

'If it's all the same to you,' Max said in a surly voice, 'I've had a long day . . .'

'Just do what I say, son.'

They walked in silence, side by side, to Valley House. Max had so many questions, but his fury at the unfairness of the situation had returned and he was too angry to ask anything. Hector could do the talking, if he wanted to.

Inside the house, they walked along the hallway. The photograph of the man who looked like Max appeared to watch them as they walked past him. Max felt a curious urge to stop and talk to the photograph, as though it was a real person. But he followed Hector who, to Max's surprise, led him into the room on the left that he had scolded Max for entering a couple of days ago.

The room hadn't changed. It was musty, the thick curtains still covered the window, and comfortable, squashy furniture was dotted all around. The painting still hung above the fireplace. They stood silently in front of it for thirty seconds, until Max couldn't bear it any longer.

'Is that my dad?' he said, unable to suppress his questions. 'R.E.J.?'

'Reginald Alistair Johnson,' Hector replied. 'Reg to his mates, so Reg to me.'

'I've always been told that he and my mum died in a house fire.'

'That was the story that was circulated.'

'So how . . . ?'

'Are you sure you want to know?'

'Of course.'

'Yeah, I suppose you would.' He peered at Max and his craggy face seemed to soften slightly. 'Sit down, Max.'

'I don't want to . . .'

'Just sit down, mate. Please.'

Hector had never called him 'mate' before. It caught Max off guard. He took a seat on a nearby sofa. Hector remained standing. 'I told you I served with your dad. There's a bit more to it than that.' He seemed to be having difficulty getting the words out. Max listened silently. 'Reg was in Afghanistan. His commanding officer instructed him and his team to launch a night-time assault on an enemy compound. Reg was the first man over the wall. Turned out that the enemy were waiting for him. He was taken captive. The rest of his team were killed. Your mum, Maddy, was back in the UK. She was an army intelligence officer, looking after you on maternity leave. When Reg was taken, she left you with a friend and headed straight to Afghanistan. She'd operated there, you see. She thought she'd be able to help find him. And she did. She used her contacts to discover that he was being held in a cave system near the Pakistan border. The commanding officer launched a major operation to rescue your father. It failed. Reg was killed by enemy fire. So was Maddy.'

Max felt numb. In all the years he'd wondered about

his parents, all those wakeful nights he'd spent picturing their deaths, he'd never imagined such a story.

'It was all hushed up,' Hector continued. 'The public never get to hear about operations like that, especially when they go so badly wrong. Nothing in the papers, nothing on the news. As far as the man in the street was concerned, Reg and Maddy were written out of history.'

'No photographs,' Max said bitterly. The lack of photographs was nothing to do with a non-existent house fire after all.

'Right.' Hector nodded.

Max stared up at the painting. The painting stared back.

'So why are there pictures of him here?' he said. His voice cracked. 'That's him in the hallway, isn't it? And this . . .' He pointed up at the painting.

'I was going to have them removed when I knew you were coming,' Hector said. 'But . . . it didn't seem right. The Special Forces Cadets were Reg's baby. He founded them. He trained up the early teams. He still operated out in the field – that's why he was in Afghanistan – but he's to the Special Forces Cadets what David Stirling was to the SAS. They wouldn't exist without him. That's why my superiors had their eye on you. That's why they insisted on putting you through selection. It seems even they can be sentimental sometimes.'

Max stood up and stared at Hector. 'And you're really going to kick me out?' he said.

'I don't need to kick you out,' Hector replied. 'You were never in.'

'Then why did you bring me back up here?' Max asked angrily.

Hector looked up at the painting again and inclined his head, as if taking leave of an old friend. 'Come with me,' he told Max.

Max was inclined to ignore him and to stay here with the picture of his father for a little longer. Indeed, he still stood there as Hector left the room. But curiosity overcame him and he hurried after the older man. Hector was halfway up the stairs when Max entered the hallway. He followed. A moment later he and Hector were in the room where Woody had briefed him when Max arrived at Valley House. The parade ground was visible through the tall windows, flooded by the setting sun. Hector was standing at an old oak desk, unlocking one of its drawers with a key. He pulled out a wooden box and handed it to Max.

'Your father's medals,' he said. 'Thought you'd like to have them before you leave. Also, some photographs of your mum and dad.'

Max took the box and opened it. He glanced cursorily at the medals inside. He was more interested in the photos. There were fifteen or twenty. Mostly they showed his mum and dad in military uniform, but there were a few of them on their wedding day. A couple of them looking relaxed by a pool on holiday. The one that bit at his heart the most was of his mum holding baby Max, his dad's arm around her shoulders.

He felt himself welling up, but then steeled himself to continue his conversation with Hector. He put the box back on the table.

'Is there an SFC challenge coin in there?'

Hector nodded.

'Guess that's the only way I'll ever get my hands on one then.'

Hector shrugged.

'I did well today,' Max said.

'Yes, you did,' Hector replied.

'If I hadn't been on that team, hundreds of people would have died. Lukas, Sami, Abby, Jack . . . they weren't in a position to help.'

'No, they weren't.'

'And that doesn't change your mind?'

The question hung in the air. Hector seemed to have no answer. He walked over to the window and looked out over the parade ground. From his position by the desk Max could see Woody and Angel waiting for the other recruits.

'I remember the first badging ceremony,' Hector said. 'Your father presented the first team of Special Forces Cadets with their challenge coins. Of the original five, three are dead. Killed on operations before the age of seventeen.' He turned to look at Max again. 'Don't take it so hard, son. Life as a Special Forces Cadet is uniquely dangerous. Ask Jack.'

'I don't need to ask Jack,' Max fumed. 'I was there, remember? Disarming the bombs, fronting up to the terrorists . . .'

'And yesterday, you failed selection. Those tests were created by your dad, Max. They were designed to identify the most capable candidates. The candidates most suited for the kind of operations the Special Forces Cadets will be sent on. The candidates most likely to stay alive.'

'But today –'

'Today you did well. Yesterday you failed an exercise because you tripped on a piece of paracord. Special Forces Cadets have to be at the top of their game every day.' He turned his back on Max and looked out of the window again. 'Green Thunder will return you to Newcastle this evening. We won't meet again.'

The conversation was over. That much was clear. Max looked at the box on the table. He almost didn't take it. Somehow he felt that the medals would just be a reminder of a life that could never be his. But he knew he would regret not taking the photos. He scooped up the box and headed to the door.

He was halfway there when he stopped.

'I never told you it was paracord,' he said quietly.

There was no reply.

Max turned. Hector was still looking out of the window at the parade ground, where the sun was setting.

'I told you I tripped,' he said. 'That was all.'

'You're mistaken,' Hector said. But he sounded unsure.

'No, I'm not. There was a length of paracord stretched between two trees, and one of Lukas's chewing-gum wrappers on the ground. I decided not to mention it because I didn't want to grass on Lukas.' Max narrowed his eyes. 'But you already know that, don't you? *Don't you?*'

Hector neither replied nor moved.

'Why did you do it?' Max breathed. 'Why did you set me up to fail?'

When there was still no reply, Max approached the window. 'You've been critical of me from the moment we met. Putting me down. Telling me I can't do stuff, that I'm not good enough. But I *am* good enough. So what's the problem, Hector? Why did you decide I wasn't going to make it from the moment you set eyes on me? Why did you set up that paracord trap and make it look like Lukas did it?'

Through the window, he could see Lukas, Sami and Abby walking onto the parade ground. He could also hear a helicopter. He didn't stop to wonder what it was. All his attention was on Hector. The older man turned to face him. His face was bathed red in the glow of the setting sun. His eyes were watery. When he spoke, his voice sounded unnaturally thin.

'The commanding officer who sent your dad on that night-time assault? The guy who led the rescue mission with your mother?' He looked at the floor. 'That was me. I sent Reg to his death. I led Maddy to hers.' He stared out of the window again.

The others were standing in a line. The helicopter sound was louder.

'I was given six months' leave. The first thing I did when I got back to England was come and see you. You were five months old. I tried to adopt you, but as a single man, and a soldier . . .' He shook his head. 'It was never going to happen. I've checked up on you over the years, Max. Watched you from a distance when you were walking home from school or wandering around town. I never made contact because I didn't want to make your life more complicated or confusing. But I made a promise to myself to keep an eye on Reg and Maddy's kid. Make sure you didn't come to any harm.' He looked at Max again. 'You saw what happened to Jack,' he said. 'He's lucky to be alive, and that could have been any of you. How could I honour my promise to keep you safe, and at the same time let you join the Special Forces Cadets? When my superiors insisted on bringing you into selection, I decided there was no way I could be responsible for another member of your family putting their life on the line.'

Max blinked at him. He could barely believe what he

was hearing. 'So when it looked like I was going to pass, you set me up?'

'I looked after you.'

'By making sure I'd get sent back to my boring life?' Max was outraged. 'How is that looking after me? I *belong* here. Isn't that obvious?'

'I've made my decision,' Hector told him.

'Is that why you kept these photos from me? So I wouldn't see my parents in military uniform? So I wouldn't get the idea of joining the army like them?'

Hector inhaled deeply. He nodded.

'But that didn't work, did it? Because it's all I've ever wanted to do!' Furious, Max held up the box. 'And what would my dad say,' he demanded, 'if he was here and he knew I wanted to join the Special Forces Cadets?'

The question hung in the air. For a moment, Max thought Hector wasn't going to answer. But the older man closed his eyes again. He drew another deep breath before opening them.

'He would back you every step of the way.'

'Well, then. If he would do it, why can't you?'

There was a long, heavy silence. Hector looked like a man in torment.

'We have a saying in the military,' he said quietly, at last. 'Train hard, fight easy. It means that the tougher the training, the more likely you are to stay alive on operations. If you stay, you and your team will train harder than any Special Forces Cadets have ever trained. I will be your worst nightmare. I will push you to the limit. Then I'll push you further. There will be days when you'll hate me, and this place, more than you could ever imagine. Your life here will not be easy. It will be mentally tough and physically brutal. You will get no thanks and no praise. That's the only way I can be sure that you will survive. Because, believe me, what happened today – that was a walk in the park.' He stared out of the window. 'It's up to you, Max,' he said. 'It's your choice.'

Outside, Angel was handing Lukas a small box. Lukas opened it and removed something Max couldn't see. Woody gave Angel another box and she stood in front of Sami, saying something, before making the next presentation. Max sprinted to the door. But before he left, he looked back. 'Hector,' he said, 'thank you.'

Hector didn't answer.

Max hurtled down the stairs, taking three steps at a time. He sprinted across the hall and past the photograph of his dad. As he burst out of the front door of Valley House he saw another helicopter setting down at the landing zone, but he didn't stop to see who it was carrying. Instead, he hurtled around the side of the house to the parade ground. Angel was handing Abby her box. She and Woody watched with surprise as Max ran up to them and took his place in the line.

'Give me one of those,' he said.

Angel hesitated. Then she looked up at the first-floor window. The cadets turned to look too. Hector was there, broad-shouldered and grim-faced. For a moment he didn't move. But then, very slowly, he nodded.

Sami gave a low whistle. Abby smiled broadly. Lukas was expressionless. Max couldn't tell what he was thinking.

'I guess you'd better have this, Max,' Angel said. She handed him the box. Max opened it. It contained a shiny enamelled coin with a black-and-white insignia: a star, with two chevrons underneath and wings on either side. He took it out and turned it round. The flip side bore the letters 'SFC'.

'Welcome to the Special Forces Cadets, Max,' Angel said. 'We're glad you're here.'

Carefully, Max slid the challenge coin back in its box. Sami and Abby crowded round him. Sami slapped him excitedly on the back and Abby kissed him on the cheek. Only Lukas stayed slightly apart. When Sami and Abby had finished congratulating him, Max stepped up to the fourth member of their team. There was a moment of awkwardness. Then Lukas held out his right hand. Max took it and gripped it firmly. Lukas smiled. It was the first time Max had seen him do that.

'We were rivals before,' Lukas said quietly. 'We're brothers now.' Without warning, he embraced Max.

'Easy, big guy,' Max said in a strained voice. Lukas's grip was very strong.

'Cadets! Fall in line!' Woody's voice, normally so friendly, had an edge to it. Max, Lukas, Abby and Sami stood in a row. 'It won't have escaped your attention that we're missing a member. We've heard from Jack's medical team. He's badly concussed. There's a chance of permanent injury. We won't be seeing him again.'

The cadets watched Woody solemnly. Max couldn't help remembering Jack's bruised and bloodied face. Hector was right: that could have been any of them. It was a sobering thought.

'The Special Forces Cadets have always operated in units of five. We're glad to have Max on the team. But that still means we're down a cadet. The good news is, we've found the perfect replacement. They've just arrived.'

Max blinked heavily. The helicopter. It must have brought the fifth cadet to Valley House.

'Who is it?' Lukas said, echoing everyone's thoughts. 'You can't put people back on the team if they failed selection. They've got to be up to the job. Hector said so himself.'

A mischievous smile played over Angel's lips. 'Oh, our fifth member is up to the job,' she said. 'More than up to the job, wouldn't you say, Woody?'

It was Woody's turn to smile. 'Reckon so,' he said.

The cadets turned to see a figure approaching. It was a

girl. She looked Chinese, and had long straight hair. She had a rucksack slung over one shoulder and was looking around nervously, as if she was lost.

Max grinned. It was Lili.

'Martial arts expert, fluent in four languages, photographic memory and pretty good at thinking on her feet,' Angel said. 'Oh, and she saved everybody's lives today. She was orphaned three years ago, I'm sorry to say, but I reckon she's just what we're looking for, don't you? Why don't you all take her to get something to eat? Martha's waiting for you in the dining room.'

'Hope she likes stew,' Woody muttered. The others laughed and headed across the parade ground towards Lili.

'Hold on, Max,' Angel said.

'Er, can it wait?' Max was eager to join the others.

'We wanted to tell you something. I don't know if Hector told you anything about the history of the SFC?'

'He kind of mentioned it.'

'Well, we were part of the first cadet team.'

'The two surviving members?' Max said, remembering what Hector had told him.

They nodded solemnly. 'Your dad trained us up,' Woody said. 'So we knew him well. He'd have been proud of what you did today.'

'Thanks,' Max said. 'I appreciate it. Look, I . . .' He glanced over at the other cadets, who were crowding around Lili.

'Off you go, mate,' Woody said. 'Enjoy tonight. Tomorrow the hard work starts.'

'Yeah,' Max said. 'Hector mentioned something about that too.'

'I thought he might have done.'

Max hurried over to the others. They were a team now, and he wanted to be part of it. But as he left the two Watchers, he overheard Angel talking to her companion. There was an emotional catch in her voice.

'Special Forces Cadets, all present and correct,' she said.

Look out for more from the
SPECIAL FORCES CADETS!

Hot Key Books

Chris Ryan

Chris Ryan was born in 1961 in a village near Newcastle. At the age of sixteen he attached himself unofficially to 'C' Squadron of 23rd Special Air Service, the territorial regiment based at Prudhoe, in Northumberland. Over the next seven years he covered hundreds of miles of moor and mountain on training exercises.

In 1984 he joined 22nd SAS, the regular Regiment, and completed three tours which took him to many parts of the world on operations and exercises. He also worked extensively in the counter-terrorist field, serving as an assaulter, sniper and finally Sniper Team Commander on the Special Projects team.

Chris was part of the SAS eight-man team chosen for the famous Bravo Two Zero mission during the 1991 Gulf War. He was the only member of the unit to escape from Iraq, where three of his colleagues were killed and four captured. This was the longest escape and evasion in the history of the SAS, and for this he was awarded the Military Medal.

Chris wrote about his experiences in his book *The One That Got Away*, which was adapted for screen and became an immediate bestseller.

Since then he has written four other books of non-fiction, over twenty bestselling novels and three series of children's books. Chris's novels have gone on inspire the Sky One series *Strike Back*.

In addition to his books, Chris has presented a number of very successful TV programmes including *Hunting Chris Ryan*, *How Not to Die* and *Chris Ryan's Elite Police*.

HOT KEY BOOKS

Thank you for choosing a Hot Key book.

If you want to know more about our authors and what we publish, you can find us online.

You can start at our website

www.hotkeybooks.com

And you can also find us on:

We hope to see you soon!